# Adventures in the Grove

# Adventures in the Grove

## A Collection of Children's Short Stories

*Norm Gillam*

Writers Club Press
New York Lincoln Shanghai

# Adventures in the Grove
## A Collection of Children's Short Stories

Writers Club Press
an imprint of iUniverse, Inc.

For information address:
iUniverse, Inc.
2021 Pine Lake Road, Suite 100
Lincoln, NE 68512
www.iuniverse.com

ISBN: 0-595-26335-6

Printed in the United States of America

# Contents

## PLAYBALL!

# Who Stole the Carrots?

*Norm Gillam*

# Everyone loves carrots

Punky, Barebutt and Mother Isabel Rabbit live in a snug little burrow at the top of Fig Tree Lane, in the town of Willow Grove. They were a poor family, but then again they *were* rabbits, so what would they spend money on if they had it?

If you'd said carrots you would probably be wrong, due to the fact that rabbits don't need to *buy* carrots. Nor do any of the other furry folk of Willow Grove, as there is always an abundance of them in the big food fields to the north of the township, and they can have as many as they want for free. The word "*free*" being used loosely here, as it is quite open to interpretation, and in most cases— misinterpretation. The Willow Grove folk had no concept of business or the value of money, and just couldn't understand the reason for the farmer's angry outbursts when they went shopping on their land. One would have thought they'd be over the moon, at having the most popular crop in the land. Why would the farmers go to all the trouble of growing acres and acres of juicy carrots and other deli-cious vegetables for them in the first place, if all they wanted to do was complain like crazy when the folk came to collect?

Not surprisingly, carrots were the main diet in this part of the land. Lettuce and cabbage were also popular, and considered delica-cies, but for some reason, those treats were not as readily available as carrots.

But carrots weren't so bad, especially with Mother Isabel in the kitchen. Carrot cakes; carrot stew; carrot soup, and hot carrot pie. Mother could make them all. She just seemed to be able to turn a carrot into a gourmet meal, one hundred different ways.

Barebutt, the baby of the family, was born one minute after Punky. Unlike his big brother, who just loves roasted carrots, Barebutt has no particular favorite where food is concerned. Some folk believe he has an eating problem, but *he* doesn't think so. If it fits in his mouth he eats it. No problem. He may have been the baby, but Barebutt was almost twice the size of Punky, with puffy cheeks and a huge floppy belly. It posed quite a dilemma for Mother Isabel when it came to keeping the pantry stocked, and as a result had to send the boys shopping on days when it got too low.

Unfortunately for Punky, it was one of those days.

# A perfect Saturday

It was a glorious spring Saturday morning in Willow Grove, and despite the westerly breeze's icy kiss, Punky Rabbit knew that it was shaping up to be one of the greatest weekends ever. The sun smiled at him through his open bedroom window. He could hear the happy sound of tiny finches and canaries chirping and flitting from branch to branch, chasing each other's tails. Crows squawked out loud from the tops of the highest oaks. Squirrels chattered noisily, and bees buzzed furiously in search of pollen. All the joyous sounds and oddities of life were going on just outside his window, and soon he'd be out there amongst it—pretty soon.

Punky yawned. He lay back with his paws behind his head, and began to think about the games that he might play, and the places that still needed exploring. Planning your weekend was the key, he maintained. Maximize your playtime by analyzing the possible obstacles, and calculating the sneaky ways around them. Also, a wise rabbit will always have a good back up plan in case of rain, and while Punky truly believed that he was one of the wisest, even he couldn't predict everything.

It felt like a great day to round up the gang—Tommy Treesnake, Jacky Hare, Wendell Weasel, and that new kid from down the road Maxwell Anteater. Perhaps they would do a spot of fishing or search for pirate's treasure down by Willow Creek. Rumor had it there was a haunted house further down the creek that needed checking out. The possibilities were endless, and to put the icing onto such a perfect day, it was also the day for the Grove's great annual picnic in the woods. Yes, it was going to be the best day, and nothing could spoil it for him.

'Punky?' called a familiar voice from behind his bedroom door. 'Punky Rabbit, get your lazy behind out of bed this instant. There's work to be done.'

'Work?' gasped Punky. He then let out a relieved chuckle, thinking that he must have heard incorrectly.

'Yes, you heard correctly,' said Mother. 'Work. Breakfast is on the table. Now move yourself along.'

As far as he was concerned, "work" was one of those awful words that should never be spoken in front of children, especially on weekends.

He buried his head beneath a pillow and whispered, 'Oh no, not today. Please let it be a dream.' If he pretended to be asleep, perhaps this bearer of unbelievably bad news might go away. Something told Punky that wasn't going to happen.

Mother Isabel opened the door and poked her head into the room.

'Come on lazy bones,' she said. 'If you want to eat next week, it's off to market with you. We also need carrots to take to the picnic this afternoon.'

'But Ma. We have to dig for pirate's treasure today. There's gold by the basket full for the taking, down by Willow Creek, so I'm told.'

Mother waved two cane baskets at him and smiled. 'Well here's the baskets, but the only treasure I want to see in them is carrots. I'll place these at the front door. Make sure you close it behind you. And make sure you wear your vest.'

'Two baskets Ma?' said Punky. 'That makes for an awful lot of carrots for one little rabbit to carry.'

'Indeed, and that's why Barebutt will be accompanying you.'

'Barebutt?' he cried.

Mother smiled. 'You should be thankful that Barebutt offered to help. With two to share the work load, you'll finish the shopping in half the time.'

'Maybe,' Punky said dejectedly. 'But it'll take us twice the time to get there and back.'

Barebutt poked his head around the doorway and offered him a cheeky gap toothed grin, daring him to argue the point further with Mother.

Punky rolled over and groaned.

# Worry Wart

Thanks to the chilly breeze, Mother insisted they wear their warm woolen vests. Identical vests with black and white checks. Punky felt a little humiliated at having to dress in a carbon copy fashion with his brother. For a start, he had an image to live up to, and his peers expected nothing short of a unique fashion statement from him. It's not as if he was six months old any more. Besides, all of his friends dressed to suit the mood. What if they crossed paths with a gang of tough lizards? Who knows what might happen? He could be seriously laughed at. Did anyone think of that?

But there was no point in arguing the matter with Mother Isabel, and knowing this Punky reluctantly slipped on his vest. He and Barebutt then picked up a basket each and set off at a brisk hop.

*Oh well,* he thought as they trundled northwards towards the great food fields. *It won't be so bad. If we hustle, I guess we can muster up the carrots and be back inside two—maybe three hours tops. As long as* someone *doesn't slow me down.*

Punky glanced at his brother. He was bouncing along happily beside him. A goofy grin seemed to be perpetually plastered across his face when they were together.

Mother Isabel shouted after them, 'You take care of Barebutt, Punky Rabbit.'

'Sure Ma,' Punky replied.

'And don't you dare go near that nasty old Farmer Simms' property.' Mother's tone became increasingly serious. 'You know how he doesn't like critters on his land?'

'I know, I know,' he cried. 'Critters—gee whiz!' he huffed, and then chuckled to himself.

They hopped up to the top of the first rise from their burrow, and looked back at Mother, still standing at the front door watching them. She worried about Barebutt when he was out of her sight, and particularly when he was with Punky. It's not that she saw Punky as a bad influence, it's just that Barebutt is not as clever as all the other kids, and sometimes they'd make fun of him because of it.

Punky was the exact opposite. He was too clever for his own good Mother thought, and would try his hardest to make sure everybody knew it.

Perhaps you can understand why Mother Isabel worried so? Her only two boys both have the uncanny ability to get themselves into spots of bother. Both in different ways and neither seem able to avoid it.

Mother's worry was evident by the way she stood at the door, peering over her wire-rimmed spectacles at them as they hopped over the first rise. Her brow was furrowed, and she was holding her paws close to her heart in such a way it seemed she was dreading the moment that her babies would be out of her sight.

The boys turned and waved to her, then descended into the first valley.

# Who's the artist?

Everyone knew that the biggest and juiciest carrots could be found at the Myers' farm, so naturally, that's where they would begin shopping. It was quite a hop from the Grove, but Punky knew it would be worth traveling the extra few miles just to sink his choppers into the sweetest carrots in the land.

'Good old' Farmer Myers,' he thought aloud. 'You can shop around all you want, but you'll never find a better quality product.'

He licked his lips in anticipation and swung the cane basket happily by his side.

They bounded along green, grassy meadows, skimming the tops of undulating hills and rolling pastures. There were several small creeks and gullies on the way to the Myers' farm, but they were no major obstacles for the two nimble footed brothers. Barebutt may have been big and heavy even for a rabbit, but he seemed to be just as agile as his big brother, and was enjoying every moment of their adventure together. Although he had to take a little more care than Punky when it came to crawling under barbed wire fences.

The bare patch on his backside seemed to suggest that Barebutt wasn't just a name.

It had been almost thirty minutes since they left Willow Grove. Punky knew they were making good time, but could see that his brother was starting to tire. They stopped for a rest in the shade beneath a large weeping willow tree.

Barebutt was grateful for the pause. He huffed and puffed as he made himself comfortable in a patch of soft grass and lay back against the trunk of the tree. Punky hadn't even raised a sweat, and was too busy taking in the scenery around them to worry about resting. He never tired of looking at the scenery, and was forever in awe at all the spectacular colors that were painted onto the surface of the land to highlight the various aspects of the landscape. Even more amazing was the fact that at different times of the day and from different positions, the shades of all these colors changed dramatically. He wondered why. When he was younger, he'd heard that humans added all the various tones of greens and reds and blues into the scenery with giant paint brushes. But now that he was a year and a half old, he realized that probably wasn't the case, and that it was more likely giant bears that did it.

Neither Punky nor Barebutt had ever seen a human, and by all reports wouldn't want to. It was rumored they had six arms, two mouths and lots of sharp teeth. Punky had certainly never seen anything carrying a paint tin that resembled that. He decided to ask his teacher about it next school day. Mrs. Badger would surely know who painted the countryside every day.

# Where'd they go?

Half an hour later they were nearing the crest of the final hill before the Myers' farm. Both were now a little puffed, but Punky had an expectant smile on his face, for he knew that acres and acres of the world's finest carrots awaited them on the other side of the hill.

They stopped on top of the green, grassy hill overlooking the property. One moment they were laughing and dancing cheerfully, and the next—

Punky was frozen on the spot like a statue. His eyes opened wide in amazement, and his jaw nearly hit the ground when he realized there was something wrong with the picture below.

Something terribly wrong.

Farmer Myers' ever-reliable acres of sweet, plump carrots were gone.

Punky rubbed his eyes vigorously in disbelief, hoping it was just a mirage. He looked again, but nothing had changed.

The carrots were all gone. All that remained were thousands of holes in the ground where they had once been.

'Impossible. This—this just can't be,' cried Punky. 'It just can't.'

He threw up his paws in amazement, and stared at the empty fields below.

'Where are they? They should be right here. They're always here.'

Barebutt hopped over beside Punky and tried to comfort him by placing his mammoth arms around him. He hugged Punky tightly. After hearing a few cracks and some muffled cries for help, Barebutt felt that perhaps he had comforted Punky enough.

Suddenly, a light of understanding flickered in Barebutt's eyes. He began hopping on the spot excitedly.

'Barebutt knows what happened,' he cried. 'Barebutt just bets he knows what happened to all the carrots.'

Punky knew he shouldn't ask, but in light of the current disaster he did anyway.

'Okay, what are you thinking brother?'

'Look,' shouted Barebutt. He pointed towards the empty fields. 'The carrots fell down all them holes in the ground. Sure they did.'

That assumption was met with a stony silence. Punky wanted to laugh and tell Barebutt that it was the most ridiculous thing he had ever heard in his life. But deep down, he was somewhat envious of the fact that he hadn't thought of it first, and so said nothing.

The rabbits raced down to the carrot field and hopped about on the loose brown soil looking for clues as to the whereabouts of the missing merchandise. With noses twitching frantically, they sniffed and searched, but came up dry. Punky felt the soil with his paw. It was slightly damp, and still rather loose, which meant the carrots had only recently disappeared.

'Well, there's only one thing we can do,' said Punky, in a matter of fact sort of manner. He wiped the excess soil from his paws and placed them on his hips.

'You mean we go home with empty baskets?' asked a bewildered Barebutt.

'Heck no!' cried Punky. 'I wouldn't get any allowance for a month. No, no Barebutt, I'm afraid you will have to check every single hole.'

Barebutt's eyes widened as he scanned the vast, empty field. 'Me?' he said. 'All by myself?

'Of course,' chuckled Punky. 'Obviously I'm going to be busy with the scientific side of the investigation. A famous detective is nothing without his faithful assistant to do the legwork. Everyone knows that.'

'But there's an awful lot of holes out there,' said Barebutt, in case Punky hadn't noticed.

'Excellent observation Barebutt,' declared Punky. 'I can tell that you're well on your way to becoming a great detective.'

Reluctantly, Barebutt began the daunting task of checking every hole in the ground for the missing carrots. He began at the northern end of the field while Punky began his investigation from under a shady bush nearby. Barebutt's theory that all the carrots had fallen down the holes in the ground was both a credible and cleverly thought out idea. It was rare for Barebutt to have such thoughts, and he decided that in future if he had any more, he'd keep them to himself.

'Who wants to be a detective anyway?' mumbled Barebutt.

# Unwelcome visitor

A sudden blood chilling scream made Punky's fine, soft bunny fur stand erect.

He sat up sharply, searched for the source of the noise that woke him up so abruptly, then bounded across to where his little brother was standing about fifty yards away, holding his nose. Tears streamed down his face.

'Something bit my nose,' he cried, and pointed to the hole in the ground in front of him. 'Something's in there.'

Punky cautiously peered into the hole from a safe distance. A pair of beady little eyes stared back at him.

'Hmm, this looks highly suspicious to me,' whispered Punky. He inched closer to the hole for a better look.

A high pitched snarl began to emanate from the depths of the hole. Punky stopped in his tracks. If he knew anything at all, it was that high pitched snarls of such a nature were usually the making of some ravenous little toe biter, with rows and rows of tiny sharp teeth.

'Best we give it a wide berth and think of a plan,' he told Barebutt, backing away from the hole. 'Unexpected encounters like this can spoil your entire weekend.'

Suddenly, the unknown creature let out a high-pitched battle cry and leapt out of the hole. It's arms and legs were flailing wildly mid air, causing the brothers to be showered with brown soil.

Punky was so startled by the unusual display, he couldn't move. He stood wide eyed, and tried to peer through the cloud of dust at whatever was making all the noise.

The battle cry stopped abruptly. It was followed by another noise—a short, dull thump. Then, like a lull in a storm, all went quiet.

As if by delayed reaction, Punky began hopping around in circles, and crying out in pain. He held one foot and danced on the other. The beast had snuck up and walloped him on the foot with something very hard and heavy.

The dust cloud cleared. It was Walter Raccoon. He held a baseball bat in one of his paws, poised for another strike.

'Thieves!' he cried. 'I have you now, you low down thieves.' Walter waved the bat in the air. 'Give 'em up, or do you want some more?'

Walter suddenly settled down as he recognized the Rabbit brothers. Punky still hopped around nursing his injured paw. Barebutt's nose still throbbed.

'Dear, dear, dear,' tittered Walter. 'Punky and Barebutt. Who would have guessed?'

Walter shook his head in disappointment.

'What are you talking about Walter Raccoon?'

'Yeah, we're not thieves,' declared Barebutt.

'Oh yeah?' Walter asked suspiciously. He jumped into the air, grasped Barebutt by the vest, and pulled him down to eye level. 'Then how do you explain this then, huh, tell me?'

He fanned his arm out across the empty field.

'You better let him go Walter, or I'll wallop you real good,' threatened Punky. 'Anyway, how do we know you're not the carrot thief? You're the one who was in the hole.'

'Ah, touché,' exclaimed Walter.

He released Barebutt's vest, and straightened it out for him. He smiled awkwardly, and offered them both a humble apology for their sustained injuries, as well as complimenting them on their identical vests, and the superb choice of colors.

'What are you doing with that bat anyway, Walter?' Punky asked curiously.

'Oh, this,' Walter appeared slightly embarrassed. 'Yes, well, you see, I was on my way to collect honey from the, you know, the bee hive thing up the road, and ah,' The words seemed taped to his tongue. It was almost as if he was trying to avoid the question.

'You collect honey with a baseball bat?' asked Barebutt.

'Of course. I do it all the time.'

'How?' said Punky.

'Sure, I could explain how,' suggested Walter. 'But neither of you would understand, so what would be the point of explaining?'

'You mean you weren't going to play baseball?' asked Punky.

'What? Me? Baseball? Oh, no, dear me no.'

'Well why are you wearing that baseball outfit?'

Walter was wearing a gray shirt and trousers with a blue stripe up the legs, and a large number 4 on the back of the shirt. Above the number were the words: "Myrtle Vale Pigtails".

Walter was lost for words.

Punky giggled. 'You were going to play baseball with the girls, weren't you Walter Raccoon?'

'Okay.' Walter shrugged in resignation. 'So, the girls were short for players today. Are you happy now? I offered to fill in for the day. Is that all right with you Punky Rabbit? Is there anything else you'd like to know? Now, do you mind if we get back to the problem at hand? Thank you.'

Walter's face had turned a deep shade of crimson, which was obvious despite the covering of black and white fur. He straightened his shirt and pants, and fidgeted until he was able to compose himself once more.

'Now, the way I see it, we have ourselves a clear case of "Liftus Carrotus".'

The brothers looked stunned. 'Huh?' They said together.

'For you uneducated vermin, that means the carrots have all been stolen.'

'Stolen? Are you sure, Walter?' asked Punky.

'Oh yes indeed. It's the only explanation,' Walter replied. 'But it's not just here, it's everywhere. From Myrtlevale in the north, to as far south as Dendigo Creek. There's not a single carrot left in the whole world. I'm surprised you haven't heard.'

'Not a one?' gasped Punky.

'Nope,' replied Walter smartly. 'All gone, all stolen.'

'This is terrible,' cried Punky. 'I can't believe they've all been stolen. How do you know this for sure Walter?'

Walter smiled. 'I heard it straight from the horse's mouth, so to speak. That knowledgeable old nag Johnny Swayback came by not long before you guys. And if anyone knows carrots, it's him. If he says they're gone, then they're gone.'

Punky found it hard to believe that anyone would want to steal all the carrots in the world. Who could eat that much anyway? As far as he knew, the folk in Willow Grove and the surrounding districts were honest and hardworking. They had no reason to steal the carrots. Besides, it would take an army of critters well over a month to collect that many. And where would they put them anyway? Punky was sure that trying to hide that many carrots would definitely raise a few eyebrows, not to mention noses around the district.

'Only humans and their strange machines would be able to do such a diabolical thing,' he concluded.

'But why would anyone do that?' asked Barebutt.

'Yes,' agreed Walter. 'But more to the point, *which* human would do such a deed?'

They all stood around kicking dirt and scratching their heads, trying to think of what to do next.

Barebutt suggested they go back to Willow Grove and find Sheriff P. I. Gerbil. He'd know what to do.

'We can't do that,' said Punky. 'Saturday is P. I. Gerbil's fishing day. Anyone disturbing him on fishing days is likely to get thrown in the old caboose.'

Punky looked over towards Farmer Myers' rickety old wooden gate. It opened out onto the hard, black barren place (the animal folk in this part of the land had no idea what an asphalt road was. All they knew was that they'd better not play on it). Something on the ground caught his attention. He hopped over to have a closer look. There were two strange patterns in the dirt, about three hops apart from each other and very long. He concluded that they were either going in the gate, or going out the gate onto the hard, black barren place.

Although Punky didn't know what tire tread patterns were, they seemed familiar to him in a way. But he couldn't quite remember why. By this time the others had hopped over to see what he was looking at. Actually, only Barebutt hopped, Walter trotted very quickly.

'What have you found there?' asked Walter.

'I'm not sure,' said Punky. 'But I've seen these things before some-where.'

'Looks like two big snake tracks to me,' said Barebutt. 'Real big snakes. Do you think they stole the carrots?'

'There aren't any snakes that big round these parts,' said Walter. 'And for that we can thank our lucky stars.'

Three sets of ears suddenly pricked up as a strange whining noise was coming towards them from the south.

'Quick you guys, hide behind that tree,' shouted Punky.

A moment later, a very noisy truck rattled and bumped its way past them, heading north along the hard, dark barren place.

'What in the world?' began Punky.

'It's a bucket of bolts,' explained Walter.

'Are you sure?'

'Yes. I know about them things. I've dodged a few in my time, don't you know? Patrick Parrot speaks the human lingo, and he heard Farmer Simms call it that.'

'What does it do?' asked Barebutt.

'Besides making funny noises, I guess it carries things just like a big basket,' replied Walter. He looked at the rear of the truck as it lumbered down the road. 'Ah yes, that particular one lives at Farmer Simms' place.'

'It does? How do you know that?' asked Punky.

'Apart from the fact that I just saw him sitting inside the thing, I'm just guessing.'

Punky clapped his paws together. 'That's it. That's where I've seen those tracks on the ground before. At the Simms' place.'

'Ar, you couldn't have seen them there Punky,' said Barebutt. 'We're not allowed to go near the Simms' place. So how could you see them there?'

'I just did, okay? And don't you go blabbing to Mother Isabel.'

Ideas began forming in Punky's head. It wasn't unusual for that to happen, but this time the ideas seemed to be leading somewhere. He recognized these ideas as being probably useful, and so the mystery of the missing carrots began to unfold.

Punky's first and most important clue to the mystery was the distinct aroma of carrots issuing from the back of the truck that just went past them. Next, the strange patterns on the ground which he'd seen at the Simms' place previously (although technically, he'd never been there), were the same as those on farmer Myers' fields now. With Walter's sighting of Farmer Simms himself, and with the knowledge of how much Farmer Simms dislikes all the bush creatures, Punky came to only one possible conclusion—The world wide carrot thief was none other than—

Mr. Bunkers, the fat, rich businessman from Wilmot Crossing.

# Furry detectives

'My Mom's not gonna like this,' said Walter, as he tried to keep up with the Rabbit brothers.

'Speak for yourself,' replied Punky. 'Mother Isabel will wallop me good if we go home with empty baskets.'

'But Wilmot Crossing is almost an hour out of our way,' complained Walter. He had to call out loud, as the rabbits were quite a way ahead.

They waited on a soft, green grassy knoll for Walter to catch up.

'You don't *have* to come if you don't want to. It just means that Barebutt and I will take all the credit for finding the stolen carrots.'

Walter reached the grassy knoll and threw his bat onto the ground. He placed his hands on his hips and bent forward, sucking in air. His little eyes squinted and his tiny sharp teeth were bared menacingly, with the effort of catching his breath.

'Anyway,' he puffed. 'I'm confused. What makes you so sure that Bunkers is the thief? I would've thought all the evidence clearly pointed towards Farmer Simms.'

'That's what I thought at first too,' said Punky. He rubbed his chin thoughtfully. 'And then I got to thinking, that was too easy. What would be the point of Farmer Simms stealing all the carrots? Like, where would he put them all for a start? And what would he do with them after that?'

Walter considered this for a moment and then said, 'Maybe he'd do it just because he doesn't like us.'

'Possible...possible,' said Punky. 'But I don't think even *he'd* go that far just to spite us. No! I think this caper is bigger than all of us animals put together. Ask yourself this Walter—who do all the farmers work for around these parts?'

'Bunkers?' Walter replied tentatively.

'Right. And if someone wanted to steal all the carrots in the world, who is the only person that has big enough sheds on his land to hide them in?'

'I guess, Bunkers?'

'Okay, now we're getting somewhere.' Punky began pacing around the perimeter of the grassy knoll, seemingly deep in thought. 'Now tell me this. What is it that humans love more than carrots?'

This one had Walter comprehensively stumped, but he didn't want to appear ignorant in front of a lower link in the food chain, so he said quite confidently, 'Shallots.'

'Shallots?' Punky laughed. 'No silly. It's money. They love money more than carrots. I'm only guessing here, but I'd say that if you had all the carrots in the world, you could have all the money in the world too.'

'Oh, yes. I see where you're going with this now Punky.' Walter raised a finger into the air. 'One question though...what exactly is a money?'

'I don't rightly know, but Ma says that humans like it more than anything, and I reckon the human who'd like it most of all is fat Mr. Bunkers.'

# Disturbing news

Meanwhile, back in the town of Willow Grove the bad news had just arrived. Emergency bells were ringing loudly. Folk were running through the Grove relaying the news to all the other residents. An urgent meeting had been called at the Town Square to discuss the situation, and to form an action committee. Many of the residents had gathered at the square to hear the mayor speak. There was a nervous babble among the huge crowd, as Mayor Peter Ferret took his place behind the podium. He looked distant and confused, as did most of the other folk. The mayor wiped a handkerchief across his sweaty forehead.

'Citizens of Willow Grove,' he began. The crowd went quiet. 'I have some very distressing news.'

'You mean the picnic in the park has been cancelled?' asked an anxious aardvark.

'Yes, that is correct. But the news gets much worse than that,' said the mayor. 'There's not much point in having a picnic, when everyone's favorite food has disappeared.'

'So, it's true then?' croaked a very ugly raven from the top of a maple tree. 'All the carrots are missing?'

Mayor Ferret looked up. 'Yes, missing presumed stolen.' He called for quiet as the babble reached fever pitch. 'Citizens, at this stage I have no answers, only my promise that we will get to the bottom of this situation. Let it be known that I am offering a generous reward for any information that leads to the recovery of the carrots.'

*Very interesting* thought the raven, as it took off in full flight.

# Who's for cake?

While the town meeting was in progress, Punky had been leading his charges in a southeasterly direction. This course led them directly to the western boundary fence of old man Bunker's property.

The brave trio peered through the strands of the barbed wire fence surrounding the vast acreage.

Enormous storage sheds consumed the land. They loomed as ugly, white monsters in contrast to the colorful, picturesque country-side that bordered them. Mr. Bunkers was involved in a large variety and number of businesses, so it came as no surprise to see a large number of sheds on his land. There were twelve in all, but as rabbits and raccoons can't count, it just seemed like a lot to them. As for what was stored in these sheds, well, that was anyone's guess, but Punky was going to make it his business to find out.

'I don't know about this Punky,' said Walter Raccoon, shaking his head back and forth. 'I don't like it one bit. There are too many unknowns to contend with. Maybe we should just pack up our bats and baskets and go home.'

A disappointed look spread over Barebutt's face when he heard that.

'We can't go home without the carrots Walter, or nobody in Willow Grove will have anything to eat. Please say that you will stay and help. Please?'

Punky was surprised that his little brother was supporting one of his outlandish schemes. He tried not to let his feelings show.

'Besides,' added Punky. 'We'll all be heroes. And you know how they treat heroes in Willow Grove don't you Walter?'

Walter thought for a moment.

'Ah, no actually, I don't. How do they treat them there?'

This was a tough one for Punky, because to his knowledge there had never been a hero in Willow Grove.

'Well, I reckon they'd treat them just fine,' he said. 'Probably put on the biggest party ever—with cake and everything. Maybe even a medal.'

'Hmm, cake huh?' Walter's perspective of the situation suddenly took a dramatic twist. 'Okay, I'm back in.'

# Crazy bird

There were a number of problems facing the prospective heroes at this time. They sat on the ground in a circle outside the barbed wire fence, and tried to formulate a plan. Luckily, the grass along the bottom of the fence line was long enough to conceal them.

Punky and Barebutt's keen sense of smell told them that there were indeed carrots somewhere nearby. The three of them agreed that they were probably stored in one of the sheds on Mr. Bunker's land. But which one? There were so many to choose from. Even Punky had to concede it would be next to impossible to check out every one before nightfall.

Another set back would be Mr. Bunker's guard dogs. They were so big, mean, and ugly that Farmer Simms seemed like an angel by comparison.

They would have to think of a way to distract them, while the search of the sheds was in progress.

Walter stood up and tapped the baseball bat against his hand. 'I know how I'd like to distract them,' he said, with a twisted smile.

Just then, there was an urgent flapping sound coming from above and behind them. The rabbits looked up just in time to see a black flash streak over the top of Walter's head.

'Ouch—' he cried, diving headlong into the grass.

Walter raised his head and looked about cautiously.

Perched upon a fence post was Ragbag Raven, sitting there preening an outstretched wing, and whistling a happy tune as if nothing had happened.

Punky and Barebutt were both laughing in fits, but Walter didn't see the funny side of it.

'Hey, you crazy bird. What do you think you're doing?' he shouted.

'Sorry about the buzz, Walter old boy,' said Ragbag. He looked about as sorry as a raven could possibly look. 'I can't resist such an inviting target. Call me an opportunist.'

'Ha,' scoffed Walter. 'How about I just call you a bird brain?'

'What are you doing up this way Ragbag?' asked Punky.

'He's probably lost,' Walter snickered.

Those who didn't know Ragbag would think he was the ugliest, clumsiest, and rude bird they had ever seen. There is however, a good reason for this. You see, a few weeks ago, while foraging in one of Farmer Myers' carrot fields for worms, he was accidentally kicked in the head by Nancy the mule. Ragbag's been cross-eyed ever since. As you could imagine, double vision poses quite a problem for someone who flies for a living. Hence, the patchy skin, lack of feathers, and various other injuries to his body have been caused by either mid air collisions with other birds, slamming into trees at high speed, or nose diving into the ground.

As for being rude, well...it's true that Ragbag never looks directly at anybody when he speaks. He always looks off into the sky or back over his shoulder, or doing as he is right now—with his head stuck under a wing, pretending to preen himself. The simple truth is—Ragbag was never intentionally rude to anyone; he is just very self-conscious about the way he looks.

Life was certainly no picnic for a cross eyed raven. And his short-term prospects weren't looking favorable either. Which brings us to why he was there.

'Actually, I believe that my services may be required here,' said Ragbag.

'Is that so? Well, it was nice seeing you again Ragbag,' said Walter as politely as possible. 'But we have some very important business to take care of here. So if you don't mind?'

Walter pointed at the sky, suggesting that Ragbag might like to take off in that direction.

'Ah, hang on a minute Walter. Let's hear what he has to say,' said Punky.

'Fiddle sticks,' grumbled Walter.

Ragbag thanked Punky and nodded politely. He then gave Walter the evil eye, but it was hard to tell which one he used.

'The word on the air waves is, you carrot munchers have a problem right now,' Ragbag began.

'We do?' asked Barebutt. Somehow his mind had wandered off the issue of the moment, and he'd been daydreaming of flying kites.

'You can say that again,' Punky sighed. 'All the carrots have been stolen, and I reckon it was fat Mr. Bunkers who did it.' Punky served Mr. Bunker's storage sheds a frosty glare. 'Do you know anything that might help us Ragbag?'

'Just so happens, I know *everything* you'd want to know,' he replied.

There was a subtle, yet suggestive tone in Ragbag's voice when he answered Punky.

'You do?' Punky said excitedly.

'Sure I do. Not much gets past us ravens you know? Do you think we just fly around all day for something to do? No sir, not us. We like to know what's going on and where it's going to.'

'Oh, I get it,' said the ever-suspicious Walter. 'You know what we *need* to know, and you've come all the way here to tell us because you're *such* a nice bird, and so happy to help. Ha, double ha!'

'Well, that's exactly right Walter.' Ragbag turned his head sharply to the east. He appeared to have spotted a target. 'Excuse me for a moment gentlemen.'

Ragbag took flight from the fence post, and soared high into the air. From a distance he looked graceful, almost majestic as he spread his raggedy black wings and hovered on a gentle thermal. He then tucked his wings in tightly, and proceeded to dive at an increasing rate of knots towards his unsuspecting prey.

Luckily for the worm it was only Ragbag zeroing in on him. But, if only he'd pulled out of his dive a second or two sooner, things might have been different.

The boys watched in amazement as Ragbag cartwheeled along the ground, and then came to rest on the only prickle patch within ten square miles. Like the battle hardened trooper he is, he got up, dusted himself off, did a quick feather count, and returned to the fence post.

Nobody spoke when Ragbag returned. What could you say? Even Walter felt a pang of sympathy for the luckless bird.

Ragbag picked up where he left off as if nothing had happened.

'In a word gentlemen,' he sighed, 'I would like to make a deal—'

# Bargaining power

For all intents and purposes, Ragbag had the entire carrot eating population over a barrel. He knew exactly where the carrots were, and for a price, would not only *tell* them where they were, but would also help to collect them.

Ragbag made his offer to the boys, after which they went into a huddle to discuss it. Walter looked over his shoulder to make sure Ragbag was not eavesdropping. He knew that ravens had excellent vision (except maybe for the cross-eyed ones), but hearing? He wasn't sure.

'Sounds pretty reasonable to me,' said Punky.

'Yeah, I like the bit about the dogs too,' Barebutt said excitedly.

Walter placed a paw to his lips. 'Shush you guys. Rule number one—don't let him hear that you're too keen. Rule number two—never accept the first offer. Take it from me, he's bumped on at least a fifty percent haggling margin.'

Barebutt looked confused. But that was not unusual. Punky didn't seem too impressed with Walter's business practices, and gave him an appropriate frown.

'Watch the master,' whispered Walter. 'I'll have him begging to help us for free.'

There was a chuckle from the top of the fence post. It was quickly disguised with a cough.

Walter turned and faced Ragbag.

'We've decided that thirty worms is totally unacceptable Ragbag.'

'Oh?' replied the raven. 'What might be acceptable then?'

'Oh, I don't know. Maybe ten?'

'You insult me Walter. Twenty.'

'Fifteen?'

'Ha. I crow at such foolishness. Eighteen.'

'Sixteen?'

'Sorry Walter, but I've grown tired of your little game. The price is now thirty-five worms. Take it or leave it.'

Walter went red in the face. 'Why you—'

Punky jumped in just in time to prevent what could have been an expensive argument.

In the end, it was agreed that thirty five worms was a fair price to pay considering the circumstances. They were to be caught by Punky, Barebutt and Walter every morning (or until Ragbag regained his normal vision), and placed in a special bag provided by Ragbag. They were to leave the bag in the fork of the giant oak in Willow Grove where he would collect it when he woke up.

It seemed that the hero business in Willow Grove could turn out to be quite a chore, and Punky quickly learnt that nothing in life was free. At least there was something to look forward to. Ragbag's doctor said that his vision would return to normal one day. But until then, he would be enjoying room service.

In exchange for the daily worms, Ragbag's part of the bargain included—revealing which of the twelve sheds stored the stolen carrots, and taking care of Bunker's crazy guard dogs while the boys went to work inside the shed.

Ragbag swooshed off the fence post and flew towards Mr. Bunker's residence, which was thirty yards east of the storage sheds, which themselves were thirty yards from the fence line where the boys stood.

They watched Ragbag circle around the house a couple of times in search of the dogs. He hovered above the back verandah for a moment, stuck a claw inside his beak and let out a piercing whistle. There was an instant commotion, and a frenzied bustling from under the verandah. The dogs emerged into the open, barking and growling in unison. Heads turned every which way as they looked for the whistling intruder who disturbed their sleep.

Ragbag swooped low and brushed his claws along one of the dog's heads. He then turned and headed northwards, leading the furious barking monsters away from the homestead and storage sheds. Occasionally he turned back on them, diving and swooping, mere inches above the sharp, snapping teeth. This was just to keep them interested. *Stupid mutts* thought Ragbag. *They'll keep this up all day if I want 'em to.*

When Ragbag had led the dogs to where Punky thought was a safe enough distance, they began making their way to the shed that Ragbag had pointed out to them. They moved quickly across the open ground, carrying their cane baskets. Walter didn't have a basket, so he carried his baseball bat. He said it might come in handy.

'Never know when you might need one.'

The large green, double wooden doors were locked tight, but as luck would have it there was a hole in the wall just large enough for Punky and Walter to squeeze through. Barebutt might be a problem though. Punky looked towards the sound of the barking dogs once more before entering the shed. They were nowhere to be seen, but from the sound, they were miles away. Ragbag had done a first class job.

# Exotic carrots

Punky entered first, and pulled the cane baskets in after him. Walter went to follow him.

'No. Barebutt next,' cried Punky. 'It might take both of us to get him in. If he gets stuck, we might not be able to get out.'

Sure enough, Barebutt could only fit his head and arms through the hole.

Punky pulled, Walter pushed, and eventually Barebutt popped through the hole, landing on top of Punky. He had that custom made grin on his face, the one that seemed to say—*Gee that was fun, can we do that again?*

It was dark inside the shed, and took a minute for their eyes to adjust from being out in the bright sunlight. Punky moved about tentatively, feeling his way with outstretched paws, and shuffling along slowly. There was loose hay on the floor and a strong aroma, which suggested that the shed must have been used to store bales of hay recently. Also, and more importantly, was the inviting aroma of freshly picked carrots. Even through the smell of hay, Punky could distinguish the different grades of carrots. He'd even hazard a guess as to whose property they came from.

Smelling them was the easy part. Finding them in the dark was proving to be harder than first thought.

They began a frantic search for the carrots. With noses twitching excitedly, they were so engrossed in their work, neither had noticed that Walter Raccoon was missing. From the opposite side of the shed came a peculiar scratching sound. Then another, and yet another. The rabbits froze. Watching, sniffing, listening.

Had they been discovered? Was it fat Mr. Bunkers? Or perhaps the two dreadful dogs had caught Ragbag, and were scratching at the door to get in. *No, that can't be it,* thought Punky. He could still hear the dogs barking off in the distance.

Suddenly, a bright burst of orange flame erupted from where the scratching sounds were heard. This was followed by the sight of a gentle yellowish glow that seemed to be floating in the air and coming towards them. They were mesmerized by the glow, and the multi-colored aura that surrounded it.

'Look what I found guys,' Walter cried triumphantly. The sound of his voice broke the spell, and the rabbits breathed a sigh of relief.

Walter had found a candle mounted on a saucer and some matches on a table on the far side of the shed.

By the light of the candle, the mystery of the stolen carrots unfolded before their very eyes. They saw thousands of wooden boxes stacked from floor to ceiling, from one end of the shed to the other. All full of delicious carrots.

Nobody had ever dreamed that there were this many carrots in the entire world, let alone in Mr. Bunker's shed.

'Will you look at that?' gasped Walter. He let out a long, slow whistle.

'It's true—it's true,' cried Barebutt. 'You were right all along Punky. Mr. Bunkers really *is* the carrot thief.'

'Right you are Barebutt,' Punky said proudly. 'I do believe this case is closed.'

They all set about sniffing the various boxes. Punky was trying to sort the local carrots from the out of town ones.

He spotted a box that seemed to have been deliberately set apart from all the others. He sniffed it.

'Yuck!' he cried. 'Must be some kind of foreign carrots in here.'

There were two words written on the top of the box in large, black letters:

**"DANGER DYNAMITE!"**

'They say that you know how to read human's writing Walter. Can you tell us what these here words say?' said Punky.

Walter scurried over to the box, leant over it and squinted his eyes. He held the candle closer to get a better look. It was rumored that Walter could read. That part was true. Unfortunately, it *was* just a rumor, and one that he started himself.

'Hmm—' he began. '"Foreign carrots"—that's what it says.'

'Ah, I thought so,' said Punky. 'I think we'll steer clear of these ones. They eat some strange food in them foreign parts you know?'

Punky suddenly stopped, looked about, and then placed his paws on his hips.

'What troubles you Punky?' Walter wanted to know.

'We still have one problem,' he replied. 'How are we going to get this many carrots back home again?'

'Oh dear,' cried Walter. 'With great difficulty.'

'Yes,' agreed Barebutt. 'We're going to need bigger baskets.'

Due to a stroke of luck, or as some might say—dumb luck, their problem was about to be solved for them.

A glob of hot candle wax dribbled down the candle and onto the end of Walter's paw. With a painful cry he dropped the saucer. It fell to the ground and shattered. The candle rolled along the floor and settled among some loose, dry hay that immediately caught fire. The boys watched in horror as the fire quickly spread across the floor, and began to engulf the box that contained the foreign carrots.

Despite their efforts to stamp it out, the fire spread too quickly. It hungrily ate its way through everything in its path, growing in intensity. In a matter of moments, it seemed the entire shed had succumbed to the inevitable.

'Abandon ship guys,' cried Punky.

Forgetting their baskets, they ran full steam towards the hole in the wall. Barebutt led the way. Thick black smoke was billowing upward from the boxes of carrots, and escaping through the hole in the wall. It was becoming difficult to breathe.

Punky saw that Barebutt had almost reached the hole, and had a sudden horrifying thought. What if he was to get stuck in the wall? They would all perish in the fire for sure.

But rather than slow down to crawl through the hole, Barebutt hopped faster. He let out a deafening cry over the roar of the flames.

'CALLABUNGA,' he roared, and crashed straight through the wall, leaving a cartoon silhouette of himself in his wake.

# Orange rain

Just as they made the fence line, there was a tremendous explosion that made the ground shake. A hot wave of rushing air lifted them off the ground, and deposited them into the soft grass on the other side of the fence.

The boys quickly got to their feet and looked back at the shed. It had been reduced to nothing more than scattered piles of smoking debris.

Punky pointed up into the sky. They all began jumping up and down, and shouting excitedly.

An enormous orange blanket of carrots soared higher and higher into the air. A happy and knowing smile began to spread over Punky's face as he followed the path of the flying carrots, and came to a sudden realization.

'Well I'll be,' he exclaimed. 'Hang me out to dry if they ain't gonna land smack in the center of Willow Grove.'

Barebutt spotted something being carried along with the blanket of carrots. It seemed to be flapping about wildly in the distance.

'What is it?' he asked.

'Whoops,' said Punky. 'I guess Ragbag's found a free ride back to Willow Grove.'

# Smoked carrot

It was pointless to try and tell their fantastic tale to the folk of Willow Grove.

The carrots were a blessing from Heaven it was said, and nothing Punky, Barebutt or Walter could say, would change their opinion.

Rather than being regarded a hero, Punky received several good wallopings from Mother Isabel. One for telling tales, one for getting home late, one for losing their cane baskets, and one just for good measure. Although Mother only used a newspaper to do her walloping, she rolled it up so tight that she might well have used a piece of hickory. Punky believed it achieved the same end.

And speaking of ends—

At dinner that evening, Mother Isabel gave thanks for the welcome bounty from above, and for the great new flavor which accompanied it.

Smoked carrot would be enjoyed by all in Willow Grove for the entire season to come.

Punky thought the carrots were particularly tasty that evening. And not just because of the new smoked flavor either. A smile touched his lips as he thought about fat Mr. Bunkers.

After dinner, Mother called the boys into the sitting room.

'Now, sit down and make yourselves comfortable,' she said.

'Ah, if it's all the same to you Mother, I think I'll stand,' said Punky. He rubbed his backside gently.

'I would like to tell you a story...and this is for you especially Punky,' said Mother. 'It is called, "The rabbit who cried wolf."'

Punky glanced at Mother sheepishly. He then looked over at Barebutt and gave him a wink.

Barebutt winked back at him, smiling delightedly.

*Ah well,* mused Punky. *So much for the hero's welcome and cake. All things considered though, it really did turn out to be the best Saturday ever.*

# Time to Fly A Kite

*Norm Gillam*

# Just a little bear

My name is Madison D Bear.

"The little bear with the big attitude", says Kulken, my best friend in the whole world.

I guess you're wondering what the 'D' stands for? Well, I'm only going to tell you this because I like you.

"Dixibell." Now that we have that out the way, I'd appreciate if you would forget it.

I'm just an average, everyday brown bear, and maybe a little small for my age. My Dad says it doesn't matter how small I am because I have a big heart, and that's what counts. I don't quite understand what that means yet because I'm only five years old, but I'm sure he's right.

What really counts *I* think, is having a best friend called Kulken who is a big, strong black bear who scares bullies away, and can carry heavy toys around.

Apart from family, friends and toys, my favorite thing in the whole world is food. In particular peanut butter and strawberries, but not at the same time. Ice cream is right up there too.

I think Kulken's red baseball cap is cool. He calls it his lucky cap, don't ask me why. Sometimes he lets me wear it, but it falls down over my eyes and I can't see where I'm going.

I *used* to like flying kites, until the day something happened.

Something big.

This major event in my young life took place about thirty eight years, three months and sixteen days ago. The funny thing is—I'm still only five years old today. Now, I'm not very good at math yet, but even my limited knowledge tells me that doesn't work out. I'm sure you're thinking the same thing.

I would like to share my amazing story with you, but first there's something you all should do before turning the next page—

Go ask your mom for a bowl of chocolate ice cream. A big one. Smother it with chocolate sauce and chocolate sprinkles. Lots of chocolate, because believe me—you're going to need it.

# Oh bother

It was an absolutely perfect day for flying kites and taking picnics in the park. Kulken carried all the heavy stuff, including the picnic basket that contained all of our favorite things, and also the stuff our Moms' put in.

The sun sparkled over Evergreen Park and the birds sang loudly, as if for our personal entertainment. Thinking back though, they may have been actually scolding us for intruding in their park. It was enjoyable anyway.

Bunches of fluffy, white clouds spotted the brilliant blue sky, and were being nudged along by an encouraging breeze. Kulken was anxious for the breeze to pick up just a little more, so that we'd have optimum kite flying conditions. He was confident it would because his nose told him so. And if a bear's nose tells you something, you better believe it. We use our noses for much more than just sneezing and getting stung by bees.

While waiting for the breeze to strengthen, Kulken concentrated on putting his kite together. It looked pretty complicated to me, and as much as I tried to help, I just got in the way. Maybe it was the frown on Kulken's face when I tried to put the round peg in the square hole, or the grunt when I tangled the kite rope that made me think that. He didn't say anything though, because he's such a nice guy, and the smartest bear I know. He builds all his own toys, so I guess he didn't need my help anyway.

I decided to take a hike down to the stream and stay out the way for awhile. It wasn't far, and perhaps a dip in the cool water would be nice.

A family of salmon was playing a ball game in the middle of the stream. It looked like fun.

'Hi,' I called. 'My name's Madison, can I play too?'

'Sure,' said one of the fish. 'Come on in.'

As I approached the stream, a salmon jumped out of the stream and squirted water in my face. They all laughed and swam away.

'Humph!' I grumbled, and shook the water from my face.

That wasn't very friendly I thought. Even the slithery earthworms were laughing at me.

I walked a little way up stream along the green, grassy bank and noticed an elderly beaver painting a picture of the woods. He looked like a friendly old beaver, and a very fine artist, I thought. His painting was vibrant with color, and very lifelike. He held a paintbrush in one hand, an artist's palette in the other, and was humming cheerfully to himself while he painted. I was careful not to make too much noise as I approached, so as not to startle him, and was about to say hello when—

I surely wish I hadn't stepped on that twig and frightened the old beaver. As he turned around, the palette full of paint fell to the ground, and his brush streaked a big yellow splotch on the picture, and quite where it wasn't supposed to be I'm certain.

The old beaver looked aghast.

'Look what you've made me do, you—you—bear!' he cried. 'One more stroke and I was finished my finest work ever.'

'I'm sorry mister, I'm sorry,' was all I could think of to say, as I quickly backpedaled down stream. The beaver's arms were waving wildly, and his was muttering to himself angrily as I disappeared from view.

I couldn't seem to do anything right that day. The harder I tried, the worse I made it for myself.

Could this day possibly get any worse?

I was about to find out.

# Help

I trudged back towards the park feeling very dejected. My eyes were down watching my feet kick leaves out the way as I walked.

Suddenly I heard a noise from above. I looked up and saw branches swaying and the sound of leaves rustling. Hmm, I thought. The breeze is picking up.

My eyes opened wide and I realized what that meant. 'Oh boy, the breeze is here,' I cried out.

I sped through the clearing in the trees and back towards the park, where I heard Kulken calling my name. He sounded excited, and no wonder. The kite was already airborne, with Kulken guiding it like an ace pilot. It soared like a majestic golden eagle, the fabric rippling as the wind carried it higher and higher into the blue sky.

Kulken began trotting along the length of the park, paying out the rope as he went. He wore a satisfied grin.

'Look at it fly,' he cried.

'It's excellent Kulk,' I replied, running along beside him.

The wind rose higher and then suddenly changed direction. It blew Kulken's lucky red cap right off his head.

It was about this moment that my roller coaster ride through life began.

Kulken let out a gasp of surprise, and made a desperate grab for his cap with one paw. The wind had blown it out of reach and was carrying it towards the trees down by the stream.

'Madison,' he cried. 'Take the rope, I have to get my lucky cap back.'

Well, I did just that, and for the first few seconds everything was fine. I watched Kulken frantically chase his red cap, which was being yanked just out of his grasp as if the wind was toying with him.

Then I started to feel very light on my feet. So much so that I could see nothing but air between them and the ground. Granted, I'm a small bear, but this was ridiculous.

But as I was being lifted off the ground and swept into the wild blue yonder, my nose decided to speak to me for the first time. Can you guess what it told me?

*You're in big trouble Madison.*

Boy, what a time to find a voice.

# Don't panic.

Understandably, many thoughts raced through my mind as I was being towed through the air, with nothing between the ground and me but a frayed old kite rope.

I only wished I'd had some of these thoughts while I was still on firm ground, where they could have been of some use to me.

Why didn't I chase after Kulken's cap myself?

Why didn't I let go of the rope as I passed over the stream?

Why didn't I just stay in bed today?

Yes, they were all good questions, and I promised myself that one day when I wasn't quite so terrified, I might try to answer them.

The air was cool against my face, and the wind whistled in my ears. I clutched the rope tightly and chanced a look down at the ground. The landscape was rapidly shrinking away. Above, I saw nothing but blue sky and the face of Kulken's eagle kite looking down at me.

I didn't panic; I was a brave little bear, but my arms were starting to tire, and blisters began to form on my paws from the rope. Dangling from a kite rope a thousand feet above the ground will do that to you.

What options did I have? Apart from letting go of the rope and taking my chances, I couldn't think of many. Besides, I wasn't feeling very lucky right then.

In the Willow Grove Wood Cubs we were taught all sorts of great things like: how to survive in the wilderness; how to find food and water; how to light a fire and what to do if dangling from a rope a thousand feet up?—I don't think so. But I did learn to tie knots, and that is the one lesson I paid attention to that might just save my furry hide.

I took three deep breaths and took one paw off the rope. Reaching below, I pulled up the loose end of the rope, made a loop and tied it off above me. Now I had a makeshift seat and could relax my tired arms.

The air was much colder the higher I climbed, and icicles began to form on my fingers, nose, whiskers and toes. It became difficult for me to move my paws.

Clouds tickled my toes as they passed below me, and under different circumstances, it might have been kind of nice. One of my friends from school once told me that clouds were big blocks of ice floating in the sky. I didn't know any different at the time (but deep down I suspected ice didn't float in air), and boy am I glad he was wrong, because I believe that I'd be as flat as a pancake now if it was true. I'd passed through big, white fluffy ones, and they didn't hurt a bit. Now that I was way, way up, dark, angry looking clouds swirled around me, making the kite bounce and weave. I don't mind admitting that that was even scarier than a hive full of angry bees.

All I could do now was sit back, try to enjoy the ride and wait for something to happen. I looked up at the face of the golden eagle above me, confident that the sturdy kite would deliver me safely wherever we were going; a tribute to Kulken's kite building skills and attention to detail.

The eagle appeared to be winking back at me, as if trying to reassure me that everything would be okay.

Winking? A picture painted on a kite can't wink at you—can it? Maybe it's the altitude and my mind was playing tricks on me.

That's when I realized I was about to have one of those moments, when you think everything's going to be okay; that inevitably signals the onset of some major disaster.

Indeed—the face of the eagle painted on the kite was not winking at me; rather, a small rip had developed in the kites' fabric across the eye, which made it look like it was winking. The small rip developed into a larger rip, accompanied by a loud tearing sound.

I watched in horror as Kulken's kite started flapping in the breeze, and it, along with me dropped out of the sky.

# What are you?

All I remember is that the world went black. I must have fallen asleep. I don't know how that was possible, but I'm glad I did because it felt like the worst nightmare I'd ever had.

I woke up in a strange place, and my first thought was to close my eyes again, as the nightmare had evidently not finished yet. I must admit though, the soft rug I awoke on was quite comfortable. Bright white light streamed out from all directions, and I had to squint my eyes against it. In the background were the funniest noises I'd ever heard. Ticking noises; whirring noises; the sound of springs springing and spronging.

I rubbed my eyes and shook my head.

A man looked down at me. He seemed very concerned and also a little confused. The long, white coat he wore had pockets in the front, filled with pencils and all kind of tools. I could see a notebook in one. Enormous spectacles hooked around very big ears, and sat awkwardly on his long thin nose, making his eyes look large and comical. Apart from some licks of gray hair above his ears, he was quite bald.

'The weary traveler awakens. Do you have a name?' he asked, opening a notebook and pulling a pencil from behind his ear. 'I certainly hope you are house trained, as I just mopped the floor.'

'I'm Madison D Bear,' I replied. 'Please don't ask what the D stands for.' A sliver of humiliation then crossed my face. 'And, yes, I'm house trained.'

'This is most irregular,' said the man. 'Do you bite?'

'Only when I'm hungry,' I said with a grin.

He made some notes in his book. 'We don't have time for bears to just drop in like this you know? You'll have to leave immediately of course.'

'Where am I and who are you?' I asked the funny looking man.

'You don't know?'

A bell started ringing in the background. The man gasped, turned and ran away.

'I'm the Timekeeper,' he shouted back. 'And I don't have time to be talking to you.'

He ran off towards the sound of the bell.

I stood up and looked around. It was like a castle and looked just like one from out of my favorite storybook. The walls and floors were covered with white tiles and were spotlessly clean. A royal red carpet ran the full length of the room and branched off towards all the clocks that lined the walls from floor to ceiling. Large clocks, small clocks, all different shapes and sizes, thousands of them complete with shiny springs and cogs, tick, tick, ticking away endlessly.

Am I dreaming? I wondered. Many arched windows were set into the walls along the length of the castle, in spaces between the clocks. I walked over to one and looked out. Nothing but—but sky. How strange. The castle appeared to be floating along on a giant white cloud.

I was determined to find out how I got here, but more importantly how to get back home again. Hopefully, the funny man with the large spectacles will be able to help me.

The man was very busy pulling levers and muttering.

'Dear, dear, dear,' he said to himself. I tried to keep up with him as he ran back and forth pulling this and pushing that. Making adjustments to all the clocks.

'Can you help me get back home mister?' I asked hopefully.

'What?' he muttered. 'Oh, deary me no. No time for that. Too much to do.'

He ran off towards a clock that started making a ting, ting, twang sound, produced an oil tin from one of his large pockets, and squirted a spring until it stopped making the noise.

'But you must help me,' I insisted. 'I'm just a little bear. I'm lost and my Mom will be worried if I'm not home for dinner.'

The Timekeeper was having some difficulty pulling a lever down.

'Here bear, lend a hand would you?'

I hopped onto the end of the lever, and together we pulled as hard as we could. It gave a grunt and a squeak, and finally it moved. The man wiped some sweat from his brow and sighed.

'Yes, I can see your predicament,' he said at last. After rubbing his chin thoughtfully for some time he added, 'Perhaps I can help. After morning tea, of course.'

I shared a spot of tea, crumpets and honey with the Timekeeper, during which he explained how I arrived at his castle. I didn't much care for the tea, but drank it anyway to be polite. The crumpets were totally awful, however the honey was first class, so I licked all the honey off and tossed the crumpets over my shoulder when the Timekeeper wasn't looking. I managed to polish off the entire bowl of what I considered to be the best honey in the whole world.

The Timekeeper explained that he'd heard a thump at his back door and went to investigate. He'd been quite cross at the time because he thought it was the Weatherman throwing hailstones at his door again. He does that kind of thing all the time I found out. Well, imagine the surprise when he found me instead, curled up asleep on his mat, with the tattered remains of the kite on top of me.

Luckily for me the Timekeeper's cloud just happened to be passing below me when it did, otherwise I may not have been here today to tell my story.

The Timekeeper had a very important job. One small slip-up and time all over the world can be thrown into disarray. *And we don't have time for that,* says the Timekeeper man.

He said that his "*Boss*" doesn't like slip-ups. Every time he mentioned his "*Boss*", he raised his eyes towards the heavens. I looked up when he did it, but all I could see was the ceiling. His "*Boss*" must have been a pretty angry guy, that's all I can think.

Morning tea was over quickly and once again the Timekeeper ran back and forth along the huge walls of clocks, making more adjustments and taking notes. He must be the busiest person in the entire universe. So how was he going to find the time to help me I wondered?

Just then a door opened into the clock room, and out marched a big eared elf like creature carrying Kulken's kite. His pointy shoes jingled as he walked, and he wore the largest smile I'd seen on any creature.

'Gobbolin—meet the bear,' said the Timekeeper.

The elf offered me a huge toothy grin, and held out the kite for inspection.

'Now,' said the Timekeeper, large eyes sparkling. 'Our special glue should've taken care of this nicely, eh Gobbolin?'

He gave the Timekeeper the thumbs up.

'And the *Boss*—' they both glanced up. 'Doesn't know?'

Gobbolin made a circle with his finger and thumb, and winked at the Timekeeper. He then bowed to me and walked back out the way he'd come. I watched after him, quite amused.

'He works for me occasionally,' the Timekeeper explained. 'Doesn't do a bad job, and he's not big on small talk.'

The kite was as good as new, and the Timekeeper man said I would be on my way back home in no time.

Well that sounded fine to me, but a couple of questions came to mind; possibly important ones.

Where was home? And how do I make the kite take me there?

'It's going to take some tricky adjustments,' said Tic Toc man referring to his notebook. 'But I believe I can have you on a strong breeze direct to Willow Grove—'

I jumped up and down and punched the air. 'Yes,' I cried.

'Of course,' the Timekeeper continued. 'That will be in exactly thirty eight years, three months, sixteen days, four hours and sixteen minutes.'

He snapped the notebook closed and looked down at me cheerfully.

My heart sank.

# Homewardbound

'Goodness me,' moaned the Timekeeper. 'If the *Boss* finds out, I'll be peddling time pieces in Frosty Land for the rest of my days.'

There was a way for me to get home, however the Timekeeper would be placing his job on the line to do it. It meant bringing time forward to the exact moment when that precise breeze would carry me back to Willow Grove. Once I was back home, time could then be returned to normal.

It sounded easy enough. The Timekeeper said it was, and that he had done it before. But the calculations had to be exact; if any one little thing went wrong it could spell disaster for the entire world.

I sure didn't want to be responsible for any disasters; nevertheless, I was only five years old and wanted to go home.

'Onward and upward then,' cried the Timekeeper.

He strapped me into a new harness that Gobbolin had made, and attached it to the kite. The new harness came with extra straps, which would enable me to steer the kite to a good landing site when the breeze delivered me to Willow Grove.

I stood at the castle's front doorstep waiting for the countdown to launch. The Timekeeper held the kite above my head. Looking over the edge of the doorstep, I saw nothing but air, and the occasional cloud floating far below. I felt a little wonky, and tried not to look down.

'I shall have you home by dinner young Master Bear,' the Time-keeper shouted triumphantly. He looked at a stopwatch in his hand. 'Precisely one minute to lift off.'

Gobbolin came running down the hall and out the front door. He held a small knapsack out to me. I took it from him and looked inside. It contained a bag of crackers and a large jar of the world's finest honey.

'For the trip home,' said the Timekeeper man.

I was so happy I felt like crying. After thanking them both, I set the knapsack into position on my back and prepared to take off.

The Timekeeper counted down the last few seconds for me, and as expected, the breeze was right on time. The kite began to flutter; a cold wind rushed against my face making my fur stand on end.

'Jump Master Bear,' cried the Timekeeper. And after a helpful nudge from Gobbolin to get me started, that's exactly what I did.

'Fly like the wind. Fly like the wind, Madison D Bear.' I heard the Timekeeper shout as I sailed away. Looking back, I smiled and waved to the Timekeeper and to Gobbolin.

It was both a happy and sad day for me. Happy because I was on my way back home, and sad because I believed I'd just seen my two new friends for the first and last time.

I had the funniest feeling that nobody would believe my fantastic tale about the Timekeeper and Gobbolin, yet they would always be a fond memory for me.

# Whoops

Whoever said, "Flying's for the birds", must be nuts. I just had the most sensational experience of my life, and enjoyed every moment of the flight home. I bet I'm the world's first flying bear. Perhaps I'll go down in the history books, who knows?

The breeze took me right back to Willow Grove, just as the Time-keeper said it would. I spotted what I thought was Evergreen Park, and steered the kite in for a perfect landing.

I'm sure it was the park, yet the grass was dried out, yellowed and harsh under my feet. The trees and stream were there as they were this morning, but something was different about the whole place. I couldn't quite put my finger on it, but—oh well, I was home now, and I'm sure Kulken would be excited to hear my fantastic story.

Something was playing on my mind and I couldn't shake it. As I unhooked the kite's harness, I wondered where all the people were. I was sure that if a little bear was whisked away into the air and had been missing all that morning, the entire community would be out searching the area by now. It's not like that sort of thing happened every day in Willow Grove.

Maybe Kulken is so busy searching for me himself that he hasn't had time to alert anyone else? But that's not like him, because he's the most responsible person I know.

I shook my head and marched down to the stream. Apart from the need for a drink of water, I thought I'd leave the kite and knapsack under a tree while I walked back to town. It was all very heavy for a little bear.

And now something else bothered me. Why are there fewer trees at the stream now than this morning? And the ones that are here look like they've been dead for many years. If I needed any further confirmation that something was amiss, then all I had to do was look into the stream. The normally full flowing, crystal clear water had been reduced to a meager trickle. I could see no fish. It must have been this way for quite some time, as the usual soft, muddy bank was now rock solid.

What had happened? Where were all the birds? Why had the water dried up? Was there any doubt that this was Willow Grove?

No, not in my mind, but it certainly was not the same Willow Grove I left behind that morning.

I stowed the kite and knapsack firmly in the fork of a tree and followed the bank of the stream down into the Grove. The twisting and turning trail seemed unfamiliar to me, although I'd traveled it hundreds of times in the past. My pace quickened as the urge to see my Mom and Dad increased. I needed them to tell me everything was all right, and I needed a big hug.

# I didn't do it

At Timekeeper castle, things were not exactly running like clockwork there either.

Sickly puffs of black smoke hiccuped from the insides of one very ill timepiece. Smoking bits and pieces were strewn across the normally spotless white floor. Amongst the debris was an arm from the Timekeeper's giant spectacles.

The Timekeeper was speechless. Remnants of his long, white lab coat now tattered and charred, lay at his feet; huge spectacles swung from one ear.

With hands raised in the air questioningly he cried, 'Great stars above, what have we done Gobbolin?'

Gobbolin immediately spun around shaking his head and pointing at himself as if to say—*What do you mean we*?

'And what has become of poor Madison D Bear?'

Gobbolin shrugged his shoulders, and wiped a tear from the corner of his eye.

They both froze like statues as the rumbling began. Heavy footsteps trudging down a creaky staircase at the far end of the clock room could only mean one thing—

The Timekeeper and Gobbolin looked at each other, and then slowly raised their eyes towards the heavens.

The *Boss* was coming.

# Home Sweet Home?

I scaled the bank of the stream adjacent to the old wooden bridge, on the outskirts of Willow Grove. I could see the main street of town from this position. Any fears I'd had up to this point that the Time-keeper man had made a mistake were soon put to rest. My first glimpse of Main Street convinced me he'd made a real whopper.

Many new houses had popped up since I'd passed through that morning. Not new houses as such, because they all had that lived in kind of look as though families had grown up in them over the years. People walked up and down the street going about their business; kids yelled and screamed as they played chase, or hide and seek. Some played marbles in the dirt patches that were once soft green grassy parks. Dogs barked from under porches, and any other niches that afforded any form of scanty relief from the burning sun. Birds chirped unhappily from the few remaining trees in the town. Large round tanks had sprung up everywhere, and I could only guess that they were there to store water.

Life seemed somewhat less than normal in the little town of Willow Grove, and I suddenly felt lonely and scared. This morning I knew everybody in town, this afternoon, I didn't recognize anyone. This may have been my town, but it was definitely not my time.

My first step onto Main Street resulted in a collision with a shiny red thing on wheels. Attached to it was a young badger. His name was Binghamton.

'Hey, watch where you're goin' will you?' he said to me crossly, brushing dust off his clothes. 'My Mom just bought this scooter for me, now the wheel's all bent.'

The kid picked up his red scooter and surveyed the damage.

In a way the machine looked familiar to me although I'd never seen one before. A word was written on the frame in yellow letters. *Madison*. I knew it was my name because that's about the only word I knew how to spell.

I apologized to Binghamton for allowing him to run over me.

'Ah, that's okay,' he said with a wave of his hand. 'Mr. Kulky will fix it for me.'

At first, I was so interested in Binghamton's scooter that the name he'd just said didn't mean anything to me.

'Where did you get this from?' I asked.

The kid pointed up Main Street. 'From the toy shop up there.' He began pushing the scooter back the way he had come. The front wheel wobbled. I did a quick damage check on myself and was pleased to find only a few minor scratches and bumps from the collision.

Then I recalled why the scooter seemed so familiar to me. It might have been as far back as forty years or it may have only been this morning, but one thing's for sure; I remember where I'd heard about scooters and from whom.

'Hey kid,' I shouted, 'Who did you say would fix your scooter?'

He looked around. 'Mr. Kulky.'

'He makes toys?'

'Kulken the toyman makes the best toys in the world,' Binghamton rolled his eyes and shook his head. 'Wow, where you been man?'

# Seeing is believing

It was the most fantastic shop I'd ever seen. The kind that every kid dreams about. Every kind of toy you could think of lined the shelves on the walls from floor to ceiling. The wooden counter was a hand crafted work of art in itself; the shop and everything in it felt just like Kulken. His fussiness about details, and expert craftsmanship was evident in every toy.

Kulken the Toyman, the sign on the shop front said. I smiled as I realized there could never have been any other outcome. Regardless of time, place or circumstance, Kulken was a toyman from start to finish, and bringing joy to all the kids through his work was what he did; was what he'd always do.

I rang a little silver bell on the counter top and waited. A shadow fell across the doorway from out back of the shop, and a shuffling noise preceded the sight of a huge black bear walking through the doorway. He was old by my books, but looked gentle and kindly. He wore a long work apron and a battered old, red baseball cap, which reminded me of Kulken's lucky cap. I thought at first it might have been his dad, but I wondered why he would be wearing Kulks' cap. He smiled and looked at me uncertainly for a long moment before speaking.

'What can I do for you today young man?' he asked pleasantly. 'Need something fixed?'

Goosebumps tingled up my spine as I looked into the old bear's eyes. I felt as though I'd known him forever. I asked to see Kulken and once again he gave me that unsettled look.

The bear placed a completed toy wagon in a vacant spot on a shelf.

'I haven't seen you round these parts before,' he said. 'But I feel like I should know you. Do I know you son, or maybe your daddy?'

'I'm Kulken's friend, Madison D Bear,' I said. 'And it's very important that I speak to him.'

There was a crash. The toyshop rumbled; toys rocked precariously on shelves when the big black bear fell to the ground.

# Ooh what a headache

I knew without further doubt, the big, black bear was my old friend Kulken. A moist cloth against his forehead helped to relieve the headache when he awoke. Kulken lay on a sofa and listened while I tried to explain who I was, and what had happened on that day so many years ago, which was still today to me.

He either didn't believe me or couldn't understand what I was saying, because he kept reminiscing about the old days; about his friend Madison, and the adventures they had together. How Madison disappeared into thin air one day, and that how a simple gust of wind changed the fortunes of so many people.

Somehow I had to make him believe that it was Madison speaking to him now, and make him understand the trouble I was in.

Kulken pointed to a new scooter standing in the shop window.

'We talked about this invention of mine near on forty years ago,' he began. 'I called it the Madison scooter after him.'

I listened politely while Kulken talked. He spoke of the many changes that were conceived from that fateful day. The weather pattern suddenly went into disarray, bringing not a drop of rain to Willow Grove since. No rain meant that there was not enough water for the stream. All the fish had packed their bags and headed for the streams in the surrounding hills of Dudevale and Myrtel Vale, which had not been affected by the change in the weather. Most of the bird life had also gone off to greener pickings, and who could blame them? Water had to be carted in every week from the neighboring towns, and stored in the big round tanks that I saw on my way into town. Willow Grove I discovered, was little more than a tourist attraction to the rest of the world. "Come see the town that Mother Nature turned her back on," they'd say; and they'd come.

Kulken lived on the top floor of his toyshop. It was comfortable, clean, and decorated with furniture he'd built himself. He invited me to share a meal of fruit and honey, for which I was most grateful. Hunger had snuck up and overtaken me. I ate everything on my plate, right down to the last cherry and asked for more.

We discussed what had happened that morning; I told him about the kite tearing; about the world's finest honey; Gobbolin; the Timekeeper man, and about the chance he took to enable me to come home again. I know that Kulken wanted to believe my story, and perhaps in a way he did. He sounded very interested in the part about the honey, but there must be a way to prove it to him I thought, and also a way to put things right again.

'Oh, silly Madison,' I cried. *Show him the kite, let him taste the honey.* Yes, that would prove everything I thought, but before I could suggest it to Kulken, we were both surprised by an urgent rapping on the window.

We turned to the window and gasped.

# A visitor

To see someone knocking on Kulken's upstairs window is strange in itself, and given the fact that there is no balcony or outside stairs for anyone to climb to be able to knock on the window in the first place made it even more peculiar.

Something peered through the window, with hands cupped around a pair of big, round eyes. It wore a long coat, and had a floppy hat pulled down over its ears. Kulken stared out the window, uncertain whether he should put on his best growl for the creature, or take a dive under his bed and hide.

A pair of pointy ears suddenly sprung out from under the hat, and a large set of teeth appeared forming a tailor made grin that could belong to only one person.

'Gobbolin!' I cried, running to the window. 'Am I glad to see you!'

I reassured Kulken that Gobbolin was a good guy and that he was here to help me. Kulken cautiously opened the window and quickly stepped aside. Gobbolin popped in all full of cheer and smiles and waves.

'How did you find me?' I asked.

Gobbolin looked up at the ceiling, placed his hands to his eyes, then spread them out theatrically around him. I assumed that meant—the *Boss* sees all.

Kulken rubbed his chin, torn between what he'd seen and heard; what he was now seeing and hearing. An element of doubt was now creeping into the reality and time of which up to now he'd been quite comfortable with. Boy, he looked tired.

We all sat down and before I could ask what had gone wrong, Gobbolin went straight into hand signal frenzy.

'Oh goodie,' said Kulken. 'I love charades.'

'This is normal stuff,' I told Kulken. 'Gobbolin uses his hands because he can't speak.

Gobbolin appeared hurt.

'Excuse *me*,' he said. 'I happen to speak quite nicely thank you very much. I just think that hand signals are much more fun. Don't you agree?'

I chuckled and nodded my head in agreement.

In the rough translation of Gobbolin's hand signals which followed, Kulken and I came to the following conclusions—Gobbolin was here to make bear eat tin can, upside down on ceiling during high wind while flapping arms.

'Oh, forget it!' groaned Gobbolin, giving up. 'Madison, you must come back with me right now to straighten this mess out. The *Boss* wants to see you, and boy is she cranky.'

# Bye, see you forty years ago

Cyriella touched down on the dry and dusty surface of Evergreen Park, the moment we arrived. A gargantuan eagle was not the mode of transport I would have expected from someone like the *Boss*, but Gobbolin seemed quite happy to clamber aboard and hang on. He motioned for me hop on. It appeared that Gobbolin was eager to depart. Perhaps the *Boss* had prepared a strict time schedule for him to adhere to, one in which he was loath to run late.

A massive white tipped wing unfolded before me; my personal feathered staircase to a first class seat beside Gobbolin, who sat on a cushion of feathers between the giant bird's wings.

The big eagle squawked as I climbed aboard the outstretched wing. I looked back at Kulken, and he was shaking his head in amazement and disbelief. That rumbling laughter I remembered so well made his huge belly shake.

He took off his lucky cap and threw it up to me.

'Here you go young Madison, if that's who you really are. You need this more than I do.'

I took the cap and put it on.

'It really is me Kulk. You can find your kite in the fork of that tree over there.'

Kulken looked to where I was pointing and nodded his head, smiling. 'I guess I can open my mind to new things just this once.'

I called down to him and waved goodbye as we took off.

'See you forty years ago Kulk,' I cried.

And then we were gone.

Kulken started walking towards the tree I'd pointed to, then stopped.

'I don't think I need proof,' he said. 'I believe him.'

He looked up to the darkening sky and laughed again. 'I believe him.'

# Meet the "Boss"

The *Boss's* office really couldn't be called an office. A more faithful description would be an enclosed forest the size of a city, complete with orchards of fruit and nut trees. A river of white water rapids gushed down the middle of the office, and ended up as a distant waterfall. Wooden shelves lined the interior walls for as far as the eye could see, and were jam packed with hundreds of thousands of jars of the world's finest honey. Soft, soothing sounds from nature seemed to be surrounding us and coming from nowhere and every-where at the same time. Soft sunlight filtered through giant skylights above the forest canopy, allowing a gentle warmth to permeate the area.

Wow! It was enough to send my five-year-old brain into a spin. More importantly, the preconceived idea I had as to who or what the *Boss* might have been had changed considerably in the short time I'd been waiting to meet him.

'We're in big, big trouble,' whispered the Timekeeper man. 'Speak only when you're spoken to, don't make eye contact, and whatever you do, do not show fear.'

For some reason I wasn't scared. I felt comfortable and safe in the *Boss's* office, as if I was in my own home. The Timekeeper on the other hand, looked like he had a nest of ants in his pants, and I hoped for his sake that he was wise enough to take his own advice.

We sat together on a giant sized couch beneath a shady coconut palm. The Timekeeper sat on my left, Gobbolin on my right. I sat amid much thumb twiddling. The Timekeeper wore a new white coat, but his enormous spectacles were held together haphazardly with sticky tape. I found it difficult not to giggle at him, but I thought I should at least try, considering the serious position we were faced with.

Suddenly a door burst open, somewhere at the far end of the office. Everything began to shake. The air quivered, honey jars rattled, and trees swayed. The noise was deafening. It felt like an earthquake. I looked around for a clear line of retreat and was about to make a run for it when the Timekeeper pulled me to my feet via the shirt collar.

Then the *Boss* was standing before us. A deafening silence followed and then descended upon us like a heavy mist. Any noise must have been frightened away by the immense presence of the creature right here in front of me.

The Timekeeper introduced me to the *Boss*. I wasn't surprised that he didn't refer to the *Boss* as the *Boss*, face to face.

What a pleasant surprise it was to discover that the *Boss* was none other than Mother Nature herself. Then change that from a pleasant surprise to totally over the moon when I discovered something else—

'Mother Nature's a big, old grizzly bear,' I shouted.

Timekeeper man cringed. Gobbolin hid behind the palm tree.

Mother Nature roared with good humor. She wore an apron, bonnet and gloves as though she'd been working in the garden. Throwing me a stern look she said, 'I should be quite annoyed with you young Madison D Bear, should I not? And not only for interrupting my day in the garden. And you can imagine the size of the garden I have to look after.'

I mustered the most sheepish look possible; head down; big, round eyes raised; arms behind my back, and hoped it was enough to avoid the full wrath of Mother Nature.

'Yes Ma'am,' I replied, then looked up sharply. 'Wait a minute. What did I do wrong?'

Mother Nature reached into a pocket in her apron, and pulled something out. 'Recognize this?' she asked, holding the remains of a sticky crumpet.

The crumpet looked awfully similar to the one I'd partly eaten on my last visit to the Timekeeper's castle. I nodded my head, recalling the wonderful flavor of the world's finest honey, then remembered what I'd done with it after licking all the honey off.

Mother Nature looked down at me with a stern look on her face. 'Do you have any idea how much trouble one of these things can cause?' she asked.

I thought about that very carefully, after which I was able to put two and two together and hoped the real answer was different from the one I got. A sticky crumpet I now realized, has the potential to cause a major catastrophe, if one were to toss it over ones shoulder indiscriminately, and should it land inside a delicate piece of equipment. In particular, a time piece.

The machine I broke, I discovered, was a special timepiece that regulated the weather and the different seasons in my part of the world. Which is why Willow Grove resembled a vast arid wasteland upon my return. It hadn't had a drop of rain in over forty years. Luckily, the damage I caused was totally reversible, but I had a feeling that it wouldn't go unpunished.

'Whoops.'

I glanced at the Timekeeper man. He shrugged.

'The good news is,' Mother began. 'The timepiece has been repaired. Willow Grove may now be reverted back to real time, and the normal weather patterns re-established.'

I clapped my hands loudly.

'That's tiggedy-boo Mother,' I said. 'All's well that ends well then, so they say. So I guess I'd better be on my way back home now because—'

'The bad news is,' she continued. 'You all must be punished for trying to put one over Mother Nature.'

The Timekeeper man's hands must have turned cold all of a sudden, because he started rubbing and blowing on them as if to warm them.

Mother Nature was very fair about dishing out the punishment I believe, and allowed us to help choose our own. She already knew that my part in blowing up the timepiece was an accident, for she of all people understood that bears hate eating crumpets. I felt that my punishment should be, to work on an environmentally friendly way to dispose of crumpets and other things I don't like to eat.

Mother Nature chuckled. 'That's a very good idea Madison. Now add five hundred trees to be planted in Willow Grove to that and you've got a deal.'

We shook on it.

The Timekeeper's visions of a bitterly cold winter in Frosty Land began to melt away, when he realized that the *Boss* wasn't as angry as he first thought. Because of the kindness he showed me, and the personal risk he was taking to help me get home, Mother Nature took this into account and went easy on him. For his punishment, he suggested that going without crumpets for a whole month would be sufficient forfeiture for anyone.

Mother agreed in principal, but pointed out that if he were to collect and jar her world's finest honey for a month or two as well, that would be such a nice thing to do. The Timekeeper screwed up his nose momentarily, comparing the world's finest bee stings to a winter in Frosty Land, but then smiled at Mother Nature and thanked her.

Poor old Gobbolin faired the worst. He pleaded ignorance and tried to distance himself from the whole affair, therefore felt that any punishment for his part was quite uncalled for. Unfortunately for him, that was not the kind of statement that Mother Nature was searching for here, and she advised him to take that into consideration while he was cleaning out Cyriella's stall twice daily for the next year. She also thanked him for volunteering to collect and count up all the unused hailstones for the next summer period.

# The time is right

I'd always known that bears were somehow special. Perhaps my being a bear had a lot to do with it, but deep down I knew there was more. The fact that Mother Nature is a bear herself just proves it. I longed to tell Kulken all about her, and about her exquisite brand of honey. He'll be so impressed.

Thoughts about my new friends; Mother Nature, the Timekeeper man, Gobbolin and the wonderful cloud palace they live on drifted gently through my mind when—

Someone said my name.

My eyes opened and I was back in Willow Grove, propped up against a tree beside the creek. Crystal clear water once again rushed along as it always had. The dense forest of green conifers and red cedars stood strong, tall and healthy. Green, leafy vegetation and flowering shrubs were abundant, and birds flew between the trees, singing happy tunes. The woods and water were abounding with life as it was this morning, as it always has been, and as it always should be. Everything was back to normal. I was home.

Kulken looked down at me, arms folded across his chest. He appeared slightly cross. I knew he was only pretending, because Kulken doesn't get cross.

'There you are sleepy bear,' he said. 'I've been looking everywhere for you.'

I sprang up excitedly, wanting to tell Kulken all about my amazing adventure, but the words wouldn't come. The harder I thought about it, the more difficult it was to remember exactly what had happened. Like a wonderful dream that evaporates the moment you wake up; was this all just a dream? I stood there mouth open wide, but no sound came out.

'Careful you don't catch flies in there,' chuckled Kulken. 'Oh, I see you have my lucky red cap. Where did you find it?'

I touched the cap. Without thinking I said, 'You gave it to me Kulk—'

Kulken was taken aback. 'Excuse me?' he said.

'Yes, as I was leaving—' I scratched my head thoughtfully, '—to go somewhere.'

'The last thing I remember is, it vanished into thin air, if you can believe that?'

Kulken suddenly looked optimistic. 'I don't suppose I gave you my kite as well? Because that seemed to disappear as well.'

I thought for a moment. 'Yes, I can remember,' I cried. 'It's right over there in the fork of a tree.'

Another fragment of memory surfaced as well. Stored with the kite I recalled, was a jar of the world's finest honey.

I rushed into the woods to where I thought the kite was stashed. Kulken followed. There were trees everywhere, but the one I was looking for had a uniquely shaped trunk that branched out at about head high which I would have recognized instantly. It wasn't there. It then occurred to me that the tree I placed Kulken's kite and the honey in, wouldn't be around for quite some time, as it was in the future when I first saw it.

With a sigh I said, 'It was right there.' I pointed to a clearing in the woods abounding with wild flowers of all descriptions, but no tree.

'Are you okay Madison?' asked Kulken. 'Sure you didn't bump your head or something?'

I could've used a huge bowl of chocolate ice cream right about then, but before that there was something I had to do.

Where it came from I don't know, but an overwhelming urge to plant trees came over me. In my pants pocket I found a handful of seeds, and as with Kulken's lucky cap, seemed to have magically appeared.

I spent the remainder of the weekend planting the mysterious seeds in the clearing beside the creek. Kulken thought I was turning nuts, but was kind enough to stay with me, and even helped plant them. This job was very important to me for some unknown reason, so I did the best I could.

A dark cloud hovered overhead, and just as we planted the last seed a soft pitter patter of rain began dancing on the leaves around us, and gently moistened the ground where we had just planted. Some small hailstones plopped at my feet. I began to laugh, but was unsure as to why.

Out of the blue I said to Kulken, 'Kulk, you're going to be the greatest toy man in the whole world one day.'

He smiled brightly and patted me on the back. 'Thank you Madison,' he simply replied.

In the years to come, I would take a great interest in the progress of the trees I had planted. There must have been at least five hundred of them. Whatever had happened on this very special day, I was certain had something to do with these trees, and that one-day they would help me to remember it all. My nose told me so; and you remember what I said about a bear's nose? Well—perhaps I'd have to wait thirty-eight years, three months and sixteen days to find out for sure.

But that's okay, because I have plenty of chocolate ice cream to help pass the time.

# Playball!

## Norm Gillam

# Spring time woes

Springtime in Willow Grove was a wondrous time of the year. Not only did it provide an abundance of new life and heavily stocked larders, it was also the season for the town's most popular sport—baseball.

You must understand that it was not the most *successful* sport. It was only the most *popular* sport, and that was generally the opinion of those who didn't play it.

Yes indeed. Springtime was a time for joy—unless of course, you played baseball in Willow Grove.

Perhaps a good reason for that is the fact that springtime heralds the annual baseball match between the rival communities of Dudevale and Willow Grove.

In the history of the contest, Willow Grove has never beaten Dudevale. Never come close in fact, and at the end of every match the coach always said the same thing—'There's always next year, always next year, always next year.'

As far as Punky Rabbit was concerned, next year never comes. Nor would it ever, unless they found themselves some real baseball players. And by the look of the local talent in Willow Grove this season, it seemed that next year wouldn't be coming this year either.

# How much can a coach bear?

Heartbreak Park is situated on the outer fringes of Willow Grove, and as the name suggests, is the home ground of the local baseball team, The Willow Grove Bandits.

It was originally called Glory Field, but that was years ago, before the good people of the Grove realized just how disappointing their team really was—and was likely to be in the future.

There may have been grass on the field at one time, and there might have been a coat of white paint on the boundary fence; but there is nobody in the town who can remember back that far who could confirm it.

Today it looks more like a dust bowl than a baseball field, and what distinguishes the latter from the former is the shape. There is a definite shape that some people (with a keen eye) might recognize as a baseball field.

It was Friday afternoon, the day before the big match, and the last practice session for the Willow Grove Bandits.

The players thought the team's name appropriate, as the only way they could hope to win a game, would be to steal it from the opposition.

Ten players in all turned up for the final session. The coach was pleased with the attendance, but at a loss as what to do with them all. He'd never had so many players at a training session before.

Coach Max Bear sat the boys in a circle on the dusty ground at home plate. He wore a blue baseball cap back the front, a whistle hung around his neck, and he carried a clipboard under one arm. Max at least wanted to look like a coach. He hoped it would make up for his inadequacy in the practical sense of the word.

He may not have been the world's greatest coach, and he certainly had no style or pizzazz in the way he formulated game plans; nor was he much of an inspiration to anyone in general, however, the town folk believed that Max Bear was the best man for the job. After playing on the team for the last ten years, he was considered the most experienced baseball player in Willow Grove.

There wasn't a thing Max couldn't teach you about how to *lose* a game.

In all honesty though, this year could well be the finest ever. At times Max had noticed what he thought might have been a spark of enthusiasm in the outfield at practice. Just a small spark mind you, but it was there, and bare in mind that it was often said–a small spark often precedes a big fire. Something was there this year that had been lacking for—well, had always been lacking really, but one or two of the players had improved noticeably.

Some could actually *hit* the ball this year, and others had *almost* taken a catch. And if Max wasn't mistaken, some of the players had even shown a slight interest in the game.

Well, this was it. Max had done his best for the team. Tomorrow was the big game, and the final analysis should show that the rest was up to them.

Punky and Barebutt Rabbit were among those sitting in the congested circle at home plate. Barebutt didn't play the game, although not for want of trying. He was seen to be too clumsy and uncoordinated to make it onto the team on the day, but he did make the best water boy you've ever seen. It broke Mother Isabel's heart to see him warming the bench each week. As far as she was concerned, he was every bit as talented as any other kid on the team. And you know what?—She was right. But why break up such an experienced losing combination?

Jacky Hare was the pitcher. For a little guy, he had a very strong arm. Unfortunately, it wasn't much use to him as a pitcher. When Jacky pitched, everyone ducked. It was now just a natural reaction. Everyone remembered the day Jacky pitched a ball to home plate—and knocked Sam Warthog clean off first base. Jacky realized he had a slight control problem—but he was working on it.

Wendell Weasel was the team catcher. At the moment he was covered with bumps and bruises. He'd been catching more balls on his forehead lately, than in his glove. He tried hard, did Wendell, and it seems he was stuck with the job, as no one else would volunteer for the position.

There was a respectful silence in the circle as Max attempted to instill a final thread of inspiration, and perhaps optimism into the boys. He tried to mentally prepare them for the big game as best he knew how.

Max held his clipboard tightly to his side. He eyed each player in turn.

'Put it this way guys,' he said, dabbing at his sweaty forehead with a handkerchief. 'It don't matter if you win, it don't matter if you lose. But please keep this in mind—if you lose to them Dudevale guys again, I'm gonna be hanging over Mayor Ferret's mantelpiece for the rest of my natural days, and then some.'

Max might well have been on edge at this particular time. He had good reason to be.

Mayor Peter Ferret's dream was to see the Willow Grove/Dudevale baseball trophy sitting over the mantelpiece at some stage during his term in office. As this was probably his last term, Mayor Ferret has stopped dreaming, and is now demanding to have the trophy.

Either way, come Saturday evening there will be *something* hanging in the Mayor's office overlooking the mantle piece.

Max shuddered at the thought.

# Wrong answer

It was an exciting time of the year for the people who didn't play baseball.

Not a lot happens in Willow Grove, so the big game was more or less a momentary release from their every day lives of repetitive normality. It was a time when people let their hair down, if only for a few hours, and did the sorts of things that any outsider might consider as outlandish, or even downright crazy. Things like—taking baskets of tomatoes, eggs, or over ripe fruit to the match, in order to vent their frustrations on the Dudevale team's players.

This was seen to be normal and healthy behavior in Willow Grove. Besides that, the people believed it was their right—their duty to act in such a way.

Even Mother Isabel was bitten by the bug of the festive spirit.

When Punky and Barebutt arrived home from practice that Friday evening, they found Mother preoccupied with several different projects at the same time. She was fussing about in the kitchen preparing the evening meal, as well as attending to the trays of cookies and muffins that she had cooked specially to take to the game.

She hummed an old tune as she tasted samples from the simmering pots on the hotplates, and meticulously added dashes of herbs and spices here and there.

The white frilly apron about her waist was spotted with various colors from the ingredients she had used. There were small trails of flour on the kitchen floor, and around her workbench. Some were decorated with a tiny, smudged footprint. The various inviting aromas made the boy's noses twitch with delight. Barebutt ran straight for the kitchen, while Punky collapsed into a large, soft easy chair in the sitting room. His stomach churned nervously as he pondered the probable outcome of tomorrow's game.

Mother shuffled out into the sitting room. She fumbled in a drawer for a moment and took out a candle, which she set in a holder on a small table near Punky. She lit the candle then smiled at him.

It seemed to Punky that it was light enough in the sitting room. The fireplace was well aglow, radiating a soft, but adequate light throughout. He absently wondered why Mother might light another candle. Then it dawned on him—

*Oh, I get it,* realized Punky. *Mother wants to speak to me in private. But she doesn't want to make it obvious.*

Mother spoke softly, but could not hide her enthusiasm.

'Oh it's so exciting Punky,' she began. 'I just can't wait for tomorrow to come.'

She sat lightly on the adjacent chair and searched his face, as though it might have contained some hidden wisdom that he was unaware of.

'How is the side looking this year dear?' she asked anxiously.

Punky shrugged. 'No worse than last year, I guess,' he said.

'Truly?'

'Yeah. I think we'll do—as equally as well as last year. Maybe better.'

Mother beamed delightedly. 'My word, that is wonderful news dear. It will be such a joy to watch my two babies playing side by side. And just imagine if you win the trophy.'

Punky shot a dubious eye at Mother.

'Two babies?' he asked.

Mother frowned. 'Yes, of course. Barebutt *is* playing this year?'

'Well. I don't rightly know Mother. Coach Bear decides on them things you see?'

Punky shifted uncomfortably in his chair.

'Perhaps you didn't hear my question correctly Punky?'

He should have known by now that questions of this nature from Mother Isabel, were really not questions at all. There could only be one correct answer, which was...'Oh, yeah, yeah, I'm sure he is Mother. I'm sure he is.'

Punky groaned in silent torment. As if he didn't have enough to worry about.

The sound of something smashing in the kitchen broke the tension within the sitting room.

'Barebutt Rabbit. Get your nose out of the icebox this instant,' cried Mother.

Mother Isabel turned to Punky again. She smiled sweetly. 'I am very pleased to hear that dear.'

She stood up and sighed contentedly.

'Now, let's eat.'

# Hero of sorts

It was the last innings; bases were loaded. Willow Grove was at bat. The score board showed two out, two strikes, no balls, and the team down three runs to none. It was crunch time. If anyone were going to save this game, *now* would be a very good time to do it.

Punky stood at home plate, clutching the bat tightly in his paw. A little too tightly perhaps. His palms began to sweat. He had a few practice swings. The crowd chanted his name, and urged him on enthusiastically from the stands, but Punky was oblivious to all the noise.

He eyeballed the pitcher. The pitcher eyeballed him.

Joey Hog was renowned as the fastest and most accurate pitcher in the land. He stood tall at the mound, and had an unnerving grin on his face. So far, he'd struck out everyone on the Willow Grove team at least once. His bright red uniform reflected the brilliant sunlight uncomfortably into Punky's eyes.

He squinted; spat a glob of well-chewed carrot onto the ground, and faced up to Joey Hog.

Joey wound up his pitch. He released. The ball seemed to be traveling in slow motion towards Punky. It looked as big as a melon. Punky swung his bat. Incredible as it may sound, he actually had time to adjust the bat mid swing, to meet the trajectory of the ball.

A sweet ping resounded from the bat as it met the ball.

The ball soared high into the air. It climbed over the in field, it arced over center field, and its descent carried it way over the rear boundary fence.

A four run homer. Punky had just won the game for Willow Grove. The crowd went wild. Punky danced around the diamond. He poked his tongue at Joey Hog. Joey watched in disbelief, and disgust. Team mates and friends met him as he touched down at home plate. They shouted and cheered and danced. Punky could hardly believe what he'd just done. Such a feeling of euphoria came over him, he thought he might pass out. His teammates picked him up and held him high in the air for all to see. They carried him on their shoulders, and began a lap of honor.

Suddenly, amid all the hype, Punky felt that he was losing his balance. He struggled against it frantically, but it was of no use. A frightening sensation of falling enveloped him, blocking out all other thoughts.

The ground loomed perilously, and all too quickly.

And then there was a crash. A painful crash. Punky cried out. His paws grasped at thin air for support. Then he opened his eyes.

'Ah, rats,' he cried, as the familiar surroundings of his bedroom came into view.

He'd fallen out of bed, and was tangled in an untidy heap of bed linen.

'Just a dream!'

# Miracles do happen

Heartbreak Park had a sort of carnival atmosphere about it. It was only eight o'clock in the morning and still two hours till game time, yet the ground was a veritable hive of activity.

Marquees and food stalls were being set in place, and the side show people were busy erecting the kid's amusement rides. The local kids were stringing colorful banners along the perimeter fence, displaying encouraging slogans such as "Willow Grove Bandits—Number 1", and "Go Bandits Go", "Bandits knock 'em outa the park". Typically, one said, "Hi Mom."

Stumpy Cockatoo was remarking the diamond with white paint. A lot of people wondered how he got the job. As he had only one leg, he held the paintbrush in his beak, while he hopped about painting the lines. And obviously, not very straight lines.

Reg Warthog and Marty Fox took a breather from constructing the spectator's stand. They watched Stumpy with enviable eyes.

'Probably got connections in the right places,' suggested Reg. 'If you know what I mean?'

Marty laughed. 'Would've scratched a few backs in his time, I'd say.'

It was a beautiful day for baseball, depending on which side you played for of course. The air was still, which meant that the infield and outfield fly balls could be judged more accurately. Unfortunately, this wouldn't help the Bandits, because nobody could catch a fly ball anyway. The Dudevale Demons on the other hand, would have a field day.

The cloudless sky allowed the sun to bath the countryside with its glistening beams of early morning light, enriching the already picture portrait like scenery.

In vast contrast to the surrounding area, was the dull and barren eyesore by the name of Heartbreak Park. Mother Nature might have been embarrassed. One thing was for certain though, Mother Isabel *certainly* was. The moment she walked through the gate with Punky and Barebutt, she became furious to see the neglected state of their park. Mother decided she would personally deal with those responsible for maintaining the ground, the very second the game was over. And if given a choice, one would've preferred to answer to Mother Nature, than Mother Isabel.

The boys helped Mother set up camp on a choice squat of ground, which would have an excellent view of the match. A little too close to the action for Punky's liking though. It was not as if he was afraid for Mother's personal safety, being so close and all; he just feared for the hides of any Dudevale player who might step out of line—on or off the field. It could get very ugly.

Mother opted for a fold out chair and a cushion, with provision for a small sun shade umbrella at the rear, rather than sit in the spectator's gallery. Punky placed a picnic basket on the ground beside her. It contained cookies, muffins, lemonade, sandwiches and of course—her knitting.

Once mother was settled and comfortable, Punky and Barebutt ambled to the other side of the diamond, where some of their teammates had congregated.

There was a more consistent flow of people through the gates now. Several groups preferred to claim squats as Mother did, and made themselves as comfortable as possible on the hard ground. Punky noticed that most people carried picnic baskets.

Sudden inexplicable feelings began to wash over him. It was more than just pre game jitters.

It was a felling of guilt or perhaps shame, as he watched the families walk by with happy faces all round. They come out every year to cheer the Bandits on. The remarkably faithful, and ever hopeful citizens of Willow Grove. They come in the hope that they might witness a miracle. Punky knew that the team owed them something special after all the years of disappointment, but didn't know when or how they would deliver the goods. It might just take a miracle for them to win the game today, and while it was probably a long shot, Punky believed that miracles did happen—even in Willow Grove. If only his team mates shared his confidence.

# Barebutt suits up

By nine thirty most of the Bandits had arrived at the ground. The team uniform was nothing to write home about. It was simply a gray T-shirt, and gray trousers. Some still had their black numbers on the back, but most had washed away as had the previous seasons. It had been quite some time since a new uniform had been issued.

The four umpires were there also, looking sharp and official in their white starched shirts and baggy trousers. Each had a whistle on a string around their neck. The four were in conference at the moment, but the chief was doing most of the talking. The three base umpires seemed to be doing a lot of nodding when the chief spoke, and they followed his finger obediently when he pointed to various parts of the field.

Art Skylark manned the scoreboard. He may or may not have a busy day, depending on whether the Demons take a particular liking to Jacky Hare's style of pitching. At any rate, he had a bird's eye view of the game.

The Hare sisters, Henny, Matilda and Delilah, were the Bandit's cheerleaders. If nothing else, they added a welcome splash of color to the dreary ground. Each sported a pretty golden, speckled skirt and white top. The pom poms were a combination of blue, green and yellow tassels. They made swishing sounds as the girls waved them in the air, practicing their routines.

Punky noticed Max Bear cantering through the main gates. He looked more troubled than usual. The Bandits gathered around the player's bench as Max arrived.

'Problems guys,' he panted. 'Big problems.'

Max thumbed through the pages of his clipboard with a sense of urgency.

'What's the matter coach?' They all wanted to know.

'Tommy Treesnake and Bert Nightowl,' he began, still panting. 'Had an accident last night. They can't play.'

Everyone gasped.

Tommy and Bert were the two most improved players on the team. With them, the Bandits might have had a shot. But without them—

Max explained to the players how Tommy and Bert were injured crossing the hard, dark barren place, on their way home from practice the previous evening. Seems they weren't quick enough to avoid one of those human's strange machines. Tommy had a broken arm, and Bert's right wing was in a sling. He wouldn't be flying around for quite awhile.

What are we going to do?' asked Max of anyone. He began to visualize his worst fears, and Mayor Ferret's mantle piece was not a pretty sight.

Well,' said Punky. 'Looks like Barebutt finally gets a shot.'

Barebutt was excited to say the least. He hopped about with joy shouting.

Max drew a line through Tommy Treesnake's name on the clipboard, and reluctantly placed a tick beside Barebutt's. With a sigh he said, 'I guess that takes care of one spot. But we're still one short. Does anyone have any ideas?' He looked over the team with a miserable look in his eyes. 'Any at all?'

His question was answered with scratches and shakes of heads. The Bandits had no other reserves, and they were fast running out of time.

'Looks like we run with a phantom batter,' said Max.

# Everyone loves winners

The Dudevale Demons strode onto the ground at a quarter to ten. They were welcomed by the locals with hearty boos and jeers.

They assembled at the visiting team's bench.

Each Demon carried a bright red sports bag, with the team name and logo stitched onto the side. The Willow Grove Bandits looked on enviously.

'Why don't we have great bags like that?' wondered Jacky Hare.

'We could,' said Wendell Weasel. 'If only we could win a game or two.'

'Yeah,' agreed Punky. 'Everyone loves a winner.'

The bandits watched on as the Demons began their warm up exercises. They stretched their legs, arms and backs. Some proceeded to casually jog around the field, while others opted to pair off and throw a ball to each other.

'Wow. Those Demons look pretty sharp this year,' noticed Punky.

The other Bandits nodded their heads in agreement.

'C'mon you guys,' said Max Bear. 'Don't worry about what they look like. All you have to do is give it all you've got. Okay?'

Max's words of advice failed to instill any sort of confidence into the squad.

'I wonder why they're not in their uniforms yet?' wondered Jacky Hare.

Suddenly Pete Canine the Demon's coach, cried out to his team, 'Okay guys. It's tomatoes this year. Let's suit up.'

Pete had been skulking through the crowd, and sneaking peeks into picnic baskets. He wanted the team to be prepared for the inevitable barrage of overripe fruit and vegetables that would be thrown at them. If he knew what colored ammunition everyone was packing, then at least they could dress in the appropriate colors.

The Demons dressed in bright red uniforms to mask the color of flying tomatoes. There was also a white uniform in each bag in case it had been flour bombs.

Plate umpire Jerry Polecat looked at his watch. He placed the whistle in his mouth and counted down the last ten seconds to ten o'clock.

The whistle blew.

Cheers and applause erupted from the crowd in the stands, and from around the perimeter of the field. Shouts of encouragement for the local team were rife.

Umpire Jerry Polecat called over the respective coaches for the toss of the coin.

He flicked it high into the air. Max Bear called heads just as the coin began its descent. The Bandits watched on hopefully, as the shiny coin twinkled in the bright sunlight. It landed in the dust near home plate with a dull thud.

Tails.

'Gee whiz,' mumbled Wendell Weasel. 'Great start. Can't even win a toss.'

Some of the players believed that winning the toss gave them an important psychological edge. Max Bear on the other hand, didn't think it mattered two cherries.

The Dudevale Demons opted to bat first.

The base umpires took their positions adjacent to each base. Jerry Polecat suited up in his protective armor, and stood at the ready behind home plate. He was well aware of Jacky Hare's mostly erratic pitches, and was well prepared this year.

There was an electric atmosphere around the ground. The Willow Grove players could feel it by the way their fur was standing on end. They were all nervous, and rightly so.

The crowd's overwhelming support for the local team was evident, in the way they cheered and shouted.

Punky knew that the Bandits owed them something big. They had to win this year. But how could they? The Bandits couldn't even field a complete team.

Umpire Polecat shouted out something to the teams. His words were muffled and muted by the rising din of the parochial crowd.

He removed his face guard, took a deep breath, and screamed out at the top of his lungs—

'Playball!'

# Crocodile tears

Scraggy Crocodile slithered along the muddy bank of the Unforgiven River.

He stopped and looked about cautiously, before settling down and basking in the warm sun. Scraggy was quite a distance out of his own territory, and rather tired after such a long swim.

The risks were enormous for him to be traveling to Willow Grove. He was aware of the consequences, but felt that he had the right to be there on this special day.

Today was the big game.

Surely the people would cut him a little slack. It's not as if he intended to misbehave, or anything like that.

He just wanted to watch.

All the crocodiles had been kicked out of town, and were banned from swimming within one mile of Willow Grove. The town people united to have them thrown out, due to a few petty incidents. The crocodiles were charged with scaring people, nicking eggs, and being stinky.

Scraggy believed it was a case of a few spoiling it for the many, but seeing as how he was a crocodile, he had no right of appeal. That was the law as far as Sheriff P. I. Gerbil was concerned anyway.

*I'll just lay here and watch the game. Nobody will even know I came to town.*

The Unforgiven River ran parallel to the rear boundary fence of Heartbreak Park.

From his position on the bank, Scraggy could enjoy a clear, but distant view of the match. He'd found a small clearance between tangled networks of tree roots, and overhanging bush. It offered excellent camouflage from the keen eyed spectators.

He felt safe in his niche. He also felt excited about being there, and was anxious for the game to commence.

Another feeling haunted Scraggy at this moment. One he'd suffered from in greater or lesser degrees at various times since the banishment. An overwhelming feeling of loneliness.

Scraggy sighed deeply, as he noticed some of his old school friends and neighbors sitting amongst the crowd, laughing and eating hotdogs. A tear trickled from an eye as he watched his team mates of old warming up before the game, his sadness doubled with the knowledge that he should have been there playing with them.

# A twist of fate

By some miraculous twist of fate, the Bandits had been able to keep the Demons scoreless for the first five innings of the match.

Needless to say, the Bandits hadn't scored either, but as far as anyone in Willow Grove could remember, it was the most impressive performance by the team to date.

It wasn't as though the Bandits were playing in any exceptional fashion. As a matter of fact, they looked less than ordinary out there.

The difference between the two teams was; that the Demons seemed to be defeating themselves. Many said that it was the worst run of dumb luck in the history of baseball.

In the first innings, the Dudevale batsmen looked to be suffering from a mere case of shaky start. But with each ball pitched by Jacky Hare from then on, came a new and unexplained turn of events for the Dudevale team.

They were rattled; dumbfounded.

It appeared that the early fumbles and stumbles had spread through the entire team like a contagious disease.

In the first innings, Jacky Hare pitched a ball to Andre the mountain lion, the Demon's big hitter. As expected, he struck the ball well. A little too well as it turned out. The ball soared straight up into the air. The Bandit's out fielders craned their heads back, and had to shield their eyes from the sun, as the ball disappeared into the heav-

- 103 -

ens. Andre strode around the diamond casually, thinking he'd hit another home run, while the Bandits were still looking for the ball.

'Where's the ball?' cried Punky.

Barebutt held out his paws and shrugged his shoulders in wonder. 'Dar—Barebutt thinks the ball is on the moon by now.'

Right then, Barebutt felt a thump in his glove on his outstretched paw. He looked into the glove and gasped. The baseball that Andre had hit seemed to appear from out of thin air.

This was to be the first of several miracles that would occur on this day.

Umpire Polecat looked astonished. Never before had he witnessed such a thing.

After wiping the dumbfounded look from his face, he pointed at Andre the mountain lion and cried, 'You're—Outa here.'

Buck Kangaroo smacked a fast ball over left field. He timed it perfectly. He placed it perfectly. On a normal day, he could have breezed it on to first base, hopping on one leg. But as he and every other Dudevale player would soon realize, today was not a normal day.

Buck took off towards first. It seemed he would easily make his ground, until his hind legs managed to get tangled up with his tail, and he ended up tied in knots still five yards from first base.

To add to the steadily growing list of problems for coach Pete Canine, Oswald Alley Cat couldn't hit a ball, little Jack Russell kept running the wrong way on the diamond, and Arnold Skunkmeister somehow got lost between bases, and hadn't been seen since.

The Willow Grove supporters became so excited at the prospect of actually winning a game, they decided to celebrate in the only way they knew how.

By removing the layer of tomatoes from their picnic baskets, and revealing the true ammunition they intended to use against the Demons.

Rotten eggs and flour bombs.

Amid a frenzied commotion of cheering and shouting, the Demon's bench was momentarily consumed in a foul smelling cloud of white dust.

The players hardly seemed to notice. There were a few rather more pressing concerns on their minds at the moment.

Max Bear stared at the score board in disbelief. This was quite a normal practice for Max, at the top of the sixth innings in any game. Except today there was a difference.

He'd asked for a time out, and had gathered his troops in a huddle for a last minute pep talk.

The Hare sisters entertained the crowd with a fancy routine, while the meeting took place.

There were looks of expectation on the faces of the Bandits, although somewhat confused. A unique sense of hope and camaraderie radiated around the circle, as they listened to what Max had to say.

'Do any of you guys know what's going on out there?' he asked quietly.

Nobody answered. Some shrugged their shoulders.

'Well, I want you all to keep doing exactly what you've been doing, okay?'

Punky chuckled. 'Gee coach, we ain't doing nothing.'

'Yeah,' added third baseman Walter Raccoon. 'Those guys aren't so hot. Just a bunch of bumbling losers, if you ask me.'

The insults began to fly thick and fast, regarding the Demon's big, clumsy feet, butter fingers, and apparent lack of vision.

'Okay, okay. Save it guys. We still have one innings to go,' Max Bear reminded his team. 'And in case you haven't noticed—we don't have any runs either.'

Max hated to put a damper on possibly the one and only time they'd be able to rub it in to the Demons. The game still had to be won. A tie was not good enough, even though it would be the best result ever recorded.

The huddle was about to break up when umpire Polecat walked over and spoke to Max Bear.

'I've had a protest from the Dudevale team Max,' said the umpire. He appeared to be rather uncomfortable.

'A protest?' said Max.

Umpire Polecat pointed at Mother Isabel and said, 'The little old lady has to move further away from the in field for the last innings.'

Everyone looked around at Mother. She was doing her knitting and humming, unaware that she was causing any fuss. She looked up; smiled, and waved to the team.

'What's the problem?' asked the coach.

'Seems she's been distressing the batsmen at home plate. Glaring at them; mouthing threats. You know, generally putting them off their game.'

Umpire Polecat wiped some nervous sweat from his brow, with his shirtsleeve.

Max Bear laughed delightedly. 'Did you hear that guys? Mother Isabel's scaring the big, bad Demons.'

Everyone thought it funny except Punky. He understood the truth of Max's statement. Mother's presence could well be intimidating at the best of times.

A tear of laughter trickled down Max's cheek. 'Would you like to ask Mother to shift camp?' he dared umpire Polecat.

'Not me, no way,' he replied. Polecat may have been the boss umpire out there, but he wasn't stupid. 'Someone has to ask her though.'

A sudden gut wrenching feeling came over Max Bear. His tears of laughter dried up the moment he understood why the Demons had been so far off their game.

Mother Isabel.

He also realized that, if she were moved out of sight of the Demon's batsmen, perhaps they would get their act together, and begin hitting a flurry of runs.

*Oh dear.* He thought. *Why now, so close to the end? I could almost feel that trophy in my hands. The boys could taste a nibble of victory. Why now? Why me? The mantle piece—oh dear.*

Mother Isabel didn't complain when Punky explained the rules to her. She was quite prepared to move, and was about to do so when Max Bear came charging over.

'It's okay,' he cried. 'You can stay, you can stay.' Max had a grin from ear to ear. He waved a book at them as he ran.

It was a baseball rulebook, for the Willow Grove district.

'Knew I'd find a use for this thing one day,' he said triumphantly.

He opened the book to page twelve, and held it out for Mother and the umpires to see.

'Look, it says right here, "The coach or *assistant coach* may be permitted to take the field, in the event that the team is one player short, but shall not be permitted to bat in place of said player,"—yada, yada, yada.'

Max smiled hopefully at Mother Isabel. 'Would you consider taking on the job of assistant coach Mother?'

It didn't take Mother long to decide. 'I'd be delighted,' she replied.

Max Bear jumped for joy. 'You stay right where you are Mother.'

Without considering the consequences, Max gave Mother a heart felt hug. Mother Isabel returned the gesture, and winked at Punky.

'Let's go Bandits. We've got a game to win,' cried Max Bear, as he rushed back to the team bench.

# Big hitter

Jacky Hare had grown in confidence as the game progressed, and as a result, his fast balls were pitching straight and true.

The first two Dudevale batsmen were dispatched very cheaply by Jacky in the sixth innings.

It was the final dig. Two out, and still neither team had scored. All Willow Grove needed to do was take out the third batsman. If they could do that, they were an even bet to win. With one batting session remaining for the Bandits, only one run would be needed.

That was Coach Max Bear's plan. It seemed achievable too, until Andre the mountain lion marched up to the plate once again.

There was a certain look in Andre's eyes. A determination; maybe desperation. The way he held the bat; his rigid stance; the concentration on his face, suggested that perhaps he reveled in the knowledge that all of Dudevale's hopes rested on his shoulders.

Jacky wound up the pitch. He concealed his finger grip on the ball within his glove, so as not to reveal the type of pitch he would deliver. Jacky was about to fire, when Andre stepped away from the plate. It was obviously a ploy to upset Jacky's rhythm.

Umpire Polecat called time out.

The spectators heckled Andre, and proceeded to besiege him with their remaining flour bombs and tomatoes.

Order was eventually restored. Andre faced up again.

Jacky pitched the perfect fast ball, but Andre anticipated it.

He took an all mighty swing. The ball pegged the sweet spot of the bat. A high pitched twang rang around the ground, as the ball skyrocketed over center field. It was last seen sailing over the rear boundary fence.

To the Bandits dismay, Andre strutted arrogantly around the diamond then kicked home plate, completing the home run that gave the Demons a one run lead in the final innings.

The Bandits hearts were suddenly in their mouths. The crowd went quiet.

How could the hopes and dreams of the entire district fade away so quickly? It just didn't seem fair.

Umpire Polecat called for a new game ball. As the Bandits were the home side, they had to supply the balls. There was only one spare.

'Guess I'd better go find that ball,' decided Max Bear. 'Looks like we might need it.'

'The Bandits need you here coach,' came a cute little voice from the sideline. It was Henny Hare. 'I'll find the ball for you.'

'Bless you Henny,' said Max.

She smiled cheerfully in the face of her team's probable defeat. She handed Matilda her pom poms, and then bounded across the field towards the boundary fence.

Umpire Jerry Polecat waited until Henny was clear of the outfield, before roaring—

'Batterrr—rup.'

# A tasty baseball

Scraggy Crocodile saw the hit. His jaws gaped open in amazement. *Will you look at that. What a marvelous knock. He really belted the cream cheese out of that one. I wonder where the ball's gone? They'll probably never find it again.*

Scraggy caught a glimpse of something in the air above him. It had torn through the high canopy of the tree line along the bank, and was heading directly towards him.

With no time to react, all Scraggy could say was, 'Oh gosh.' Before he felt the thump in his lower jaw.

The ball had landed in his mouth, and impaled on one of his incisors. He yelped. Scraggy thrashed about violently, trying to dislodge the ball. It stuck fast.

His legs were not quite long enough to reach the ball, which left Scraggy at a loss as what to do next. He shook his head, flapped his jaw, and even tried biting the ball off. But it was going nowhere.

'Oh boy, I'm in trouble now,' he mumbled. 'They're gonna come looking for this any minute.'

Scraggy was on the verge of slipping back into the water and heading home, when he heard the soft pitter-patter of little feet in the mud. He lay motionless, and listened. The sound was coming towards him from the south, and he could tell that it was just around a small bend in the bank.

Henny Hare appeared around the bend, and spotted Scraggy in front of her. She skidded to a halt, placed her paws to her mouth, and tried to squeal. Nothing came out.

# Saved by the scream

Two more runs had been added to Dudevale's score card during Henny's absence, before being dismissed for the final time by the Bandits.

They now led three—zip. It seemed an insurmountable lead.

It was now the last batting innings for the home side.

To make matters worse for the Bandits, the phantom batter was due early in the last dig. That meant they were already one out before anyone even stepped up to the plate.

Wendell Weasel, the Bandit's catcher, selected a bat from the cache.

His whole body ached from the battering he'd received from taking Jacky Hare's fast balls. Also, a few experimental curve balls had taken him unawares. Wendell thanked the stars for face protectors.

Without a hit that day, Wendell's confidence was understandably at a low. He appreciated the position the Bandits were in at that moment, and wished that it were anyone but him stepping up to bat. He picked up a black batter's helmet, and placed it on his head. He then waited in the circle for the umpire to call him out.

Joey Hog was acclaimed to be Dudevale's secret weapon. Although hardly a secret, he could however be described as a weapon of sorts.

Everyone knows that Joey is the biggest, fastest, and meanest pitcher in the entire league. His eyes seemed to pierce the very soul of any batter, and reduce him to little more than a quivering wreck.

Joey was brought in to pitch the last innings for the Demons.

Wendell swallowed nervously as he limped up to the plate, deliberately avoiding Joey's unsettling glare.

He could hear the noise of the crowd in the background, and smell the delightful aromas from the food stalls. Honey pies, cotton candy and fresh eucalyptus on a stick. Oh how he wished he could be a spectator right then.

Wendell shouldered the bat, and stood in position.

Joey didn't waste any time. He wound up the pitch, and delivered the ball right down the alley.

Two strikes later, umpire Polecat roared, 'You're—Outa here,' and kindly directed Wendell to the Bandit's bench.

Punky Rabbit batted next. He was able to swat a ground ball to left field, and was thus, the first Bandit to make a base hit.

Second baseman Pedro Whippet followed Punky at bat. His teammates shouted words of encouragement as he made his way to the batter's box. His shirt was ruffled, and streaked with dirt from a previous attempt at sliding into first base.

Pedro was usually very quick between bases, but unfortunately, could never place the ball well enough, in order to take advantage of it.

Joey Hog let fly with a deceptive slow ball.

Pedro mistimed it completely. The ball deflected off the top edge of his bat, and dropped gracefully into the waiting mitt of the Demon's short stop.

The supportive crowd suddenly hushed. The Bandits were two out, three runs down, and fast running out of batters.

Some of the Dudevale players ran across to the pitcher's mound to high five Joey Hog.

They could smell another victory in the air.

It was big Barebutt Rabbit's turn to bat. He was unfazed by the precarious predicament the Bandits were in. Perhaps he just didn't understand.

Joey Hog glared at Jack, in an attempt to unnerve him.

Jack smiled and waved back at Joey.

The pitcher wasn't happy. *Nobody smiles at me—and nobody waves at me and gets away with it. This guy is really asking for it.*

Joey was so angry with Jack that his lips turned up into a twisted smile, and he snarled viciously. His face burned a bright shade of crimson; his fingers dug ridges into the fabric of the ball, such was his rage at this cheeky rabbit that dared to smile at him.

Joey's anger obviously clouded his judgment, and affected his pitch.

The ball slipped out of his fingers as he delivered it, and landed on the toe of Jack's right runner.

Jack cried out in pain. He dropped the bat, and hopped about on one foot.

His pain was quickly alleviated, when umpire Polecat called out, 'Take a walk.'

Little did Jack realize he'd just opened a door for the Bandits that had earlier been slammed in their faces. For taking a blow to the body from Joey Hog, it resulted in an automatic walk to first base. This left a path wide open for the Bandit's star hitter, Angelo Lion-heart.

Angelo had to hit a home run, to tie the game.

As the phantom batter followed Angelo, there was no chance of the Bandits winning the game. A tie, although not the result the Willow Grove people were hoping for, would go down in history as the closest the Bandits had ever come to beating Dudevale.

That in itself would be something to celebrate.

But, no time for celebrations yet. They still needed to score a home run.

There was silence as Angelo stepped into the batter's box, and took his stance.

He cut the air with a practice swing, and adjusted his grip on the bat.

Punky cautiously led off second base, under the watchful eye of Joey Hog.

Angelo's golden mane glistened in the mid morning sun. His eyes narrowed to slits as he matched the stare from Joey Hog. A cast of grim determination set his face rigid, as he prepared for whatever Joey might throw at him.

The pitcher began his wind up. He checked first base, he checked second and then—

The still, silent air was shattered with the sound of a blood-curdling scream.

Everybody in the stadium froze. All eyes turned to the rear of the field.

'Henny!' cried Punky.

# Hare nabbing crocodile

The rear boundary fence of Heartbreak Park rattled and shook with the weight of so many people trying to clamber over it at once.

It seemed that every person in the stadium had come to investigate the terrifying scream.

Punky was first over the fence. He sprinted the fifty yards between the fence and the bank of the river. His shirttail flapped out behind him as he ran, and somewhere between there and second base, he'd lost his baseball helmet.

He could hear faint squeals trailing off in the distance. The sound was coming from upstream. Punky fought his way through the dense undergrowth and stringy tree vines, and burst out onto the muddy bank, just in time to see a crocodile quickly fish tailing its way upriver.

Henny was riding on his back. Punky's heart pounded.

A group of townsfolk arrived at the river just after him. 'Someone get Sheriff P. I. Gerbil,' he shouted. 'A crocodile just kidnapped Henny Hare.'

# Celebrity Sheriff

Punky, Max Bear, and Wendell Weasel hadn't waited for Sheriff P. I. Gerbil to arrive on the scene of the kidnapping. They were heading upstream by foot, in hot pursuit of the hare nabbing crocodile.

Before long, quite a crowd had gathered on the bank of the Unforgiven River. Including the local sheriff. He was not amused at being dragged away from his favorite fishing hole.

Sheriff P. I. Gerbil looked all about the bank in search of clues to Henny's kidnapping.

Being so short, and squat, and close to the ground, enabled him to recognize evidence that taller folk might easily overlook.

He raised his white stetson, and scratched his furry head.

'Hmm,' said the sheriff. 'Looksh like an open and shut case to me.'

A long, silver mustache hung down below his nose, almost covering his mouth completely. The hair muffled his words, and everyone had to listen very closely to understand what he was saying.

The sheriff turned to his deputy, Tomain Walrus. 'Warm up the shlammer Tomain, we're gonna have ourselves a guest tonight.'

Tomain threw a quick salute, and then hightailed it back to town to prepare the jail cell. As there hadn't been much call for a jail cell in Willow Grove, the sheriff had converted it into a spa, and sauna room.

'And order me a double cheese pizza while you're at it,' he added.

Someone jabbed a microphone in front of sheriff Gerbil's face. 'Do you know who the perpetrator is yet Sheriff?'

P. I. Gerbil appeared slightly confused. 'Who? The what? And just who in the dickens would you be?'

'Diehard Duck, KKKLM news.'

The sheriff straightened his shirt, and polished up his badge, even though there were no cameras to look impressive for.

'Oh, the press, heh, heh,' he muttered. 'As a matter a fack, I do.'

P. I. Gerbil moved a little closer to the microphone. He relished the thought of being heard on the radio, and felt that a smidgen of over-dramatization couldn't hurt.

'And I guarantee to you, that there'll be shum shorry critter behind bars, come night fall.'

This drew a rowdy response from the crowd assembled by the riverbank. Some applauded the sheriff's bold statement.

Diehard Duck removed a note pad from the brim of his nut brown felt hat. He thumbed through to the page he was looking for.

'Rumor has it sheriff, that one Screggy Crocodile may be on the list of suspects.'

'Scraggah Crocodile,' corrected sheriff Gerbil. 'And ah yup, he's the one I want.'

The reporter nodded his head as the sheriff spoke.

'How can you be sure that it is in fact *Scraggy* Crocodile you're looking for?'

'Looky here,' said the sheriff, pointing to some tracks in the mud. 'A toe misshing from the right front foot.'

The reporter and the other interested spectators had a close look at the tracks. A low murmur began to circle within the crowd. It seems no one had picked up on this small, but significant piece of evidence.

'Chainshaw accident, a ways back,' explained P. I. Gerbil.

'That's remarkable sheriff,' declared Diehard.

'It's what they pay me for.'

'Do you know what motivated the kidnapping of Henny Hare?'

'Revenge.'

'Could you expand on that sheriff?'

'Well—Scraggah's meaner than a rattler, and sly ash a fox. I ran him an' his whole gang out of town a time back. Reckon he's been planning this for a time, just to get back at me.'

'What charges do you expect to lay?'

'Kidnappin'; trespassin'; and disturbing my fishin' day. That's for starters.'

Sheriff Gerbil turned and faced the crowd. 'I want five good men to form ma posse,' he shouted.

Hands went up eagerly. The sheriff picked out the most suitable candidates.

'One more question sheriff,' called Diehard.

'Make it snappy,' he barked.

'Perhaps you could share with the listeners, the next steps in your investigation.'

'Ma nexsht steps?' he began. 'Ma nexsht steps are gonna be darn big ones.'

With that, the sheriff adjusted his stetson, hitched his jeans high on his waist, and began striding along the bank, heading up river.

'Let's go boys,' he called to his posse.

Sheriff P. I. Gerbil's bowed legs might have suggested he'd been riding horses for many years. But where does a gerbil find a horse of adequate size to ride? Probably in the same place he'd find a decent pair of jeans to fit. The answer is certainly *not* in Willow Grove.

Every ten yards or so, the sheriff had to stop and pull his jeans up, or suffer the indignity of having them wrapped around his ankles.

He marched on, grumbling something about the state of the clothing industry in Willow Grove.

# In hot pursuit

Punky Rabbit led the way through the murky swampland that branched off the Unforgiven River three miles north of Willow Grove.

Visibility was poor, as the tall timber top canopy screened the sunlight. Patches of light would sometimes appear here and there, as the tall trees swayed in the intermittent breeze.

Punky, Max and Wendell stepped lightly on the uncertain and unfamiliar ground.

One wrong step could plunge them all into the murky depths of the swamp.

Curlews cried out as they approached, seemingly spreading the word that intruders were entering their territory. Unidentified insects clicked; gibbered, and twitted all about them. None were seen.

Strange noises set their spines tingling. Talk was kept to a minimum, in order to stay alert. The scene was, in a word spooky.

Punky had been out here only once before. Ironically, it was to visit Scraggy, whom at the time played baseball with the Bandits, and was quite a good hitter.

But that was long ago, and under different circumstances.

Today, Punky felt unwelcome, not to mention unnerved.

His sensitive nose caught a faint whiff of smoke. A wood stove perhaps.

As he recalled, Scraggy's shack wasn't much farther ahead.

A lump grew in Punky's throat, as they walked slowly into the unknown. There were so many questions that he could not begin to answer.

Why had Scraggy kidnapped Henny? Was she hurt? Punky couldn't believe that Scraggy would do something like that. He always seemed kind of nice.

When Scraggy's shack came into view, Punky's first instinct was to rush in and drag Henny out of there.

Max Bear grabbed him by the back of the shirt, and held him back.

'Hang on there Punky,' he said quietly. 'We have to come up with a plan. Can't just go bursting in. Have to know what we're up against.'

Punky sighed, and sat down on the damp ground behind a clump of bush.

'You're right coach.' He parted some foliage on the bush, and looked through at the shack.

It was of a simple design, constructed with logs that Scraggy had found floating on the swamp. Gaps between the logs had been filled in with mud. The roof was thatched. A stovepipe was set through it, and secured at a crooked angle. Smoke wafted from it at the moment, spiraling upwards until the breeze carried it away.

Half of the shack stood on firm ground, while the other half seemed to float on the malodorous swamp water.

Max Bear pointed to the one and only window, built into the side of dwelling.

'You two wait here. I'll peek in the window, see if I can spot Henny.'

Punky considered protesting, but realized that Max was the tallest of the three. He'd have little trouble reaching the height of the window.

Max kept low, treading lightly and quietly on the balls of his feet.

He stood against the side wall of the shack, and cautiously peered into the window.

The glass was covered with grime. He couldn't see in.

Max wiped a corner of the window with his paw, and looked again.

He stood there for quite awhile, motionless.

Punky and Wendell were growing impatient, wondering what he could see.

Max stood back from the window, and turned to face the boys. He had a smile on his face.

He waved them on.

Everything must have been okay. Punky felt a rush of relief.

The three gathered at the front door. It was ajar. The sound of voices came from within. Henny, talking and giggling. Scraggy laughed occasionally. Definitely not the sounds one would expect from a kidnapper, and his victim.

Max debated whether he should knock on the door, but then he realized that Scraggy was a fugitive and not a friend on this day. He decided to just lightly push it open.

Henny and Scraggy looked around with surprise, when the three heads poked through the doorway.

They were sitting at the kitchen table. It looked like they'd been enjoying a friendly game together, as if nothing was wrong. As if they didn't realize that the whole town of Willow Grove was up in arms, and searching for them at this very moment.

Scraggy dived under the table, and tried to make himself disappear. A difficult thing to do when you're a six foot crocodile.

'Hi guys,' said Henny. 'Like a game of checkers?'

# Tea anyone?

Scraggy boiled water on the stove for some more tea.

Max Bear turned the ill-fated baseball over and over in his paw, and mused over Scraggy and Henny's bizarre explanation of the day's events. He poked a finger through the hole in the ball, still unable to believe what had happened.

The furnishings in Scraggy's shack were meager, but tasteful in a funny sort of way. A square, wooden table dominated the center of the dining room. Punky imagined that it allowed him room to move his long tail about, without knocking everything over. Two wooden chairs accompanied the table. A leg had been nailed back onto one crookedly. A long sofa backed against one wall, and was positioned beneath the window in which Max had looked through.

Framed pictures hung from the walls at various points, and a bookshelf sat against the feature wall, visible from the front door. Rather than books, the bookshelf housed old baseball photos, and a few trophies that Scraggy had earned.

The most dominating feature inside the shack was the pot bellied stove, huffing and puffing away in the section partitioned off as the kitchen.

Scraggy was about to pour the tea, when the door was kicked open.

Henny squealed.

An angry looking little creature in a large white stetson, stood in the door way with hands on hips. His long, silver mustache flew into the air with each forceful breath.

'Scraggah Crocodile,' he bellowed. 'You in a heap a trouble, boy.'

# A win win situation

Punky, Wendell and Max looked out the window. There must have been one hundred people outside Scraggy's shack, all waiting to see him brought to justice.

Sheriff P.I. Gerbil was in a hurry to handcuff Scraggy, and drag him off to jail. He believed there was still a good five hours fishing time left, if he played his cards right.

'No sheriff,' cried Henny. 'Scraggy's not a criminal.'

She stood between the sheriff and Scraggy.

The sheriff looked surprised. 'Hold on thar little misshy. Nobody comes into ma town; kidnaps one of my citizensh, and gets off shcott free.'

He tried to sidestep Henny, but she blocked him. 'But he didn't kidnap me,' Henny insisted.

'Yeah sheriff,' added Max Bear. 'It's all a big misunderstanding.'

'Mishunderstanding or not. Nobody comes into ma town; dish-turbs a my fishin' day, and gets off shcot free then.'

Henny proceeded to tell her story to the sheriff, as she had previously to Punky, Wendell, and Max Bear. She realized that the hard-headed sheriff might take some convincing though. Especially on his fishing day.

She told of her initial shock of almost stumbling over Scraggy on the riverbank, and how the missing baseball had become lodged on his tooth. It was stuck so fast that she had to strain every muscle in her body in her attempt to remove it. When the ball finally and suddenly slipped off Scraggy's tooth, it threw her off balance and into the slippery mud. She then fell face first into the murky water. Hence, the terrified scream that everybody on the baseball field heard.

Scraggy had remembered that Henny couldn't swim. He slid into the water to save her. By diving below her, he was able to get Henny onto his back, and thus, bring her to the surface.

Henny was soaking wet, slimy, and cold. She coughed and spluttered from the amount of water she'd taken in.

Scraggy had decided to brave the wrath of the town folk and carry her home, so she could dry off, and recover from her ordeal.

He would've too, had it not been for the sound of people yelling, and the sight of those people running very quickly in his direction.

He quickly came to the conclusion that, he'd better make like an egg, and scramble his way out of there. And so, with Henny on his back, he high tailed it up river to the safety of the swamp, and home.

Hmm—' Sheriff Gerbil sounded skeptical. 'You're tellin' me that Scraggah here *saved* your life?'

'Not only that,' replied Henny. 'He gave me a warm change of clothes, while he washed my yucky ones.'

'That's right sheriff,' added Punky. 'Scraggy's not a criminal, he's a hero.'

Scraggy blushed. 'Ah shucks.'

Sheriff Gerbil paced back and forth on the dining room floor. He seemed unsure of what to do.

'Can't just let you off Scraggah,' he began, shaking his head. 'You violated our one-mile limit. And beshides, I promised the good people there'd be someone in our jail, come nightfall. I'm a man of my word.'

'Give him a break sheriff,' said Wendell Weasel.

'He just wanted to watch the game,' added Punky.

Max Bear had been sitting on the sofa taking all this in. He noticed the baseball photos, and trophies on the bookshelf.

Suddenly, he jumped up and ran across to the sheriff.

'Wait a minute—wait just a dog gone minute,' he cried. 'Scraggy is still a registered player for the Willow Grove baseball league.'

'So what?' said sheriff Gerbil.

'Don't you see?' Max said excitedly. 'If Scraggy replaces the phantom batter in the last dig, the Bandits can win the game.'

Everyone in the room suddenly understood the enormity of what coach Bear had just said. They cheered collectively, and looked expectantly at Scraggy.

Without having to be asked, Scraggy said, 'By Jove's, I'll do it.'

Max Bear dropped to his knees, eyeball to eyeball with sheriff Gerbil.

Normally, Max frowned on people who groveled to get what they wanted. But today was a special day, and Max groveled just as hard as he possibly could.

'You have to let him off sheriff. Please? *Please?*'

'I don't know—I just, I, I—' The sheriff was stumped.

Max tried another angle. 'Think of the headlines in tomorrow's paper. "Brilliant piece of police work by sheriff P. I. Gerbil, results in historic Willow Grove win over Dudevale."'

Sheriff Gerbil nodded his head approvingly. 'That does have a kind of nice ring to it.'

# Bear for mayor

The Willow Grove Bandits went on to win their very first game of baseball.

As it turned out, Angelo Lionheart didn't hit that home run.

But Scraggy Crocodile did.

He was a hero in more ways than one, and the people of Willow Grove appropriately and enthusiastically welcomed him and the other crocodiles back into town from that day forward.

Coach Max Bear was also considered a hero, to the extent that the people unanimously voted him in as the next Mayor of Willow Grove.

Mayor Bear's first job in office was to find a new coach for the Bandits. To the former Mayor, Peter Ferret's horror, he was duly elected. Max advised the new coach as to what would happen, if the space now occupied by the Willow Grove/Dudevale baseball trophy on the mantelpiece ever became vacant—

Many changes were to occur in Willow Grove following that memorable day.

The Bandits were issued with brand new uniforms, bats and gloves. And—nice, shiny, red, zip up bags for everyone. The players were delighted.

A ceremony took place at Heartbreak Park, a couple of weeks after the win. The players were each given a ten-pound hammer, and told to go to work on the signboard displaying the name of the field.

In its place, a new name board was erected. "Victory Park— Home of the *new* Bandits."

The E—


Now hold on just a minute there—

Perhaps we should take a detour on our way out. Back to the Willow Grove Sheriff's office, on the night the Bandits won the game.

As we all know, the Sheriff is a gerbil is of his word. He said so himself.

He assured the Willow Grove folk that there'd be *some sorry critter* in his jail cell come nightfall.

Well guess what? He was right.

Sheriff Gerbil stood at the door to the cell, and looked through the bars. He had a wry smile on his face.

He picked up a beaten old enamel cup, and rattled it across the bars.

Bring me more hot chocolate Tomain,' he shouted.

Tomain came out from behind his desk, took the sheriff's cup, and waddled away.

'And don't forget to wake me up at six AM sharp.'

Sheriff P. I. Gerbil scrambled up onto the bottom bunk, and placed his paws behind his head.

He giggled to himself. 'Ah, such is life in Willow Grove.'

And so it was.

0-595-26335-6

Printed in the United States
94657LV00005B/168/A